DENIAL

"Stonewall it, man, they can't prove anything. . . ."

"God in heaven, man, we are the *Roman Catholic Church*, not some sleazy corporate miscreant! Dozens of priests know, I know, the Pope knows. The lawsuits will bankrupt us!"

ANGER . . .

Satan laughed. "Your subroutines are quite readable, Father De Leone. We could rewrite them if we chose. But that would ruin the experiment."

"Experiment? *Cheap blasphemy!*"

BARGAINING . . .

"Yes, I know, you're appalled. Your immortal soul might be trapped in an eternal electronic limbo. You are a dying man, Father De Leone, I give you my profuse papal blessing . . .

"But I also offer you a chance to achieve sainthood . . ."

AND ACCEPTANCE

"I'm calling you in the name of the Father, and the Son, and the Software Ghost! I call your spirit from the vasty deep!"

A ripple of something passed across the screen. Then a voice.

"Hello, Marley . . ."

Deus X

A chilling and provocative tale of a politically correct pontiff, computers, and the final frontier: death.

OTHER WORKS BY
NORMAN SPINRAD

Novels

Agent of Chaos
Bug Jack Barron
Child of Fortune
The Children of Hamelin
The Iron Dream
Little Heroes
The Men in the Jungle
The Mind Game
Passing Through the Flame
Riding the Torch
Russian Spring
The Solarians
Songs from the Stars
The Void Captain's Tale
A World Between

Story Collections

The Last Hurrah of the Golden Horde
No Direction Home
Other Americas
The Star-Spangled Future

Nonfiction

Fragments of America
Stayin' Alive: A Writer's Guide
Science Fiction in the Real World

Anthologies (editor)

The New Tomorrows
Modern Science Fiction

deus x

Norman

Spinrad

BANTAM BOOKS
NEW YORK · TORONTO · LONDON · SYDNEY · AUCKLAND

DEUS X
A Bantam Spectra Book / January 1993

ISBN 0-553-29677-9

Published simultaneously in the United States and Canada

PRINTED IN THE UNITED STATES OF AMERICA

RAD   0   9   8   7   6   5   4   3   2   1

For JEAN DALADIER

Deus X

1

They say these are the last days, Moma Gaia's been murdered by her idiot children, reefs all coral corpses, ice still going, waters still arising, biosphere melting away in the supertropic sun like a big jellyfish beached on the Martian shore.

For sure we're the grandsons and daughters of less than wise old monkeys, but on the other hand, we all made of mud, one of the good books says, so considering where we come from, maybe we haven't done too bad. And in my line of work, I've become convinced that even the entities on the Other Side are just playing the cards that someone else dealt as best they can.

I've been told that's a bad attitude, but a lot of

the people who say it pay me good money to use it for their own devices. 'Cause that's what it takes to deal with what's on the Other Side, whether you think you're dealing with electronic loas, or your dearly departed, or just the expert system ghosts haunting the bits and bytes.

Even if you believe there's nothing on the Other Side capable of feeling anything, there's plenty can model it well enough to pass any emotional Turing test, so when in postmortem Rome you better model yourself some manners, because the entities there have no trouble at all convincing *you* when your realer-than-thou attitude pisses them off.

Me, I ain't faking it, man, I may have been born into the last days, but even what's left of this sick old biosphere's still gonna be around long after I'm gone to my chosen reward.

Maybe it's the Herb that gives me a sunny spirit. Old Sol, he don't seem so friendly now without the ozone to shade our poor hides from his death-ray glare, but I say it ain't the Golden Boy who's changed, besides which, without him there's only the dark, so me, I grease myself with sunscreen, put on my old straw hat and shades, light me up a spliff, and set my course through sunlit seas.

So call me Ishmael, it's not my name, but I'd rather do the Great White Wail than join the funeral march.

My real name's Marley Philippe, and I live on

the *Mellow Yellow*. That's my boat, man, not the Herb talking, and it's as real as it gets for me. I bought her with ill-gotten gains, better you don't know, six years past, and she's still the perfected state of the art.

The *Yellow*'s a forty-foot windfoil sailer, and the foils double as solar collectors, and in the dead of night on a glassy sea she can still do seventeen knots on a full three days' charge for ten hours and run my working hardware with plenty of juice left over to give me fifty watts of traveling music. In a bad-ass hurricane, the foils deflate into the masts, the masts fold into the deck, the cockpit canopy goes up, and I can seal up a cabin with a neat little galley and a great big fridge and everything I need to stay on the Board and make like a submarine if I have to.

What more can a poor boy ask? Except of course a sea full of leaping fish and tropical islands laden with sweet fruit and dusky damsels basking in the balmy sunshine. Admittedly, that's a bit hard to come by, what with the Caribbean paradise of my ancestors reduced to a series of huddled masses clinging to highland remnants surrounded by moribund coastal swamp and all but the larger citified islands of the Pacific long since drowned in the desert sea.

But if the dumb hand of man has taken away the sunshine isles of yore, human stupidity giveth too, with the same blind chance. It giveth fjords in Scandinavia where you sail between great rugged cliffs dripping with subtropic jungle on crystal waters where refugee seals come to graze on shoals of sardines. It giveth the Great Egyptian Sea where you glide through half a thousand miles of reeds infested with birds fleeing the Central African Waste. It giveth scuba diving over the verdigreed emerald streets of New Orleans. It giveth most of all the transformational shores of the Mediterranean, where I spend the months between November and April.

With sunscreen, and straw hat, and shades, the sun's not so bad then; if you're lucky enough to be black as me, you can even enjoy it.

I like to sail through the Gibraltar Bight long about the end of October and cruise east off the northern shore, what was once called the Costa Brava and the Côte d'Azur. It's an old, old part of the so-called civilized world, mountains to the sea in some parts, coastal plains and deltas in others, and it's been accumulating interesting ruins since before the Romans started kicking Greek ass.

Most of the latest and least romantic layer, the late-twentieth-century beach strip of turista ticky-tacky that ran all the way from the Rock to Nice, is mercifully sunk beneath the rising sea, leaving only the bargetowns of the boat people floating above the drowned hotels, now refugee camps for what few fish remain in the dying sea.

Where the old coast was more rugged, the little

towns and villages retreated slowly up the cliffs as the water rose in some places, in others former clifftop towns find themselves sitting on the shore. Along the eastern shore of North America, the North Sea coast, places like that where depopulated cities huddle behind the great seawalls, it seems like a battlefront where you know who's gonna lose, but down here, the people who remain seem to have literally gone with the flow as they always have, their perpetually crumbling seacoast towns and villages rising and falling with the time and the tide.

These days I usually follow the boot of Italy about as far down as Sicily, then make the passage to the African coast. Sometimes I used to go up the Adriatic side as far as dear dead Venice to smoke the Herb among the pelagic ruins and get nice and maudlin at the noble follies of Old World Man, whose most lasting monuments are those to an endless succession of the Glory That Was.

The last few years, I haven't ventured that far; I do not like to sweat the race with the summer sun back out into the Atlantic and up to the fjords to sit out the summer in endurable climes.

Once, early on in my migratory career, I sped along my eastern course and down the Italian coast so I could swing down through the Greek islands before I had to turn back to beat the sun. Bad mistake, man. My sense of timing turned out to be muchisimo optimistic, and so did my classical illusions.

The Greek islands got it bad. When the fish died and the sun turned lethal to the tourist trade, the economy went Haitian and worse, and the die-off of the trees and ground cover did the rest, and now there's nothing left of the magic kingdom of Homeric myth but boneyard isles, abandoned now to handfuls of human ruin-rats swimming pathetically toward you with knives in their mouths and starvation in their eyes.

Black boy, don't let the summer sun rise on you here!

But it did. There were hundreds of islands still more or less rising out of the dead azure sea, not a one of them without the bleaching bones of towns and villages that were a thousand years old when my ancestors were dragged out of Mother Africa to durance vile in the American Babylon. I don't know what I was looking for as I sailed for weeks around this vast stone Sargasso of quaint seatown corpses and beautiful bleak marble monuments, too dead even for Homeric ghosts.

Whatever it was, I didn't find it. Instead, an unseasonably early rise in the ultraviolet count found me while I was still off Algeria, and I had eight days sealed in cockpit and cabin to brood on the awfulness of it all, afraid to even partake of the Herb.

I decided that I hadn't bought the *Mellow Yel-*

low to become an intrepid explorer, or to darken my skies with reminders of what this world must once have been, but to sail endlessly round as languid seas as I could find, fulfilling as best I could the ancestral dream in all those retro-Reg songs popular in the New York of my boyhood.

I want to play Columbus venturing out into deep unknown waters and wondering whether I'm going to sail over the edge into the void, I've got more than enough on the Other Side.

Fish no longer jump out of the sea into a beachcomber's net, nor can I step ashore and pluck my fill of fruit from the trees, and one has other expenses in this life, man, so even I need a job.

More jobs than not still mean going somewhere to work, which means staying somewhere to live, but the Big Board is everywhere and nowhere, and those of us who work it can sail round their chosen circuit to their hearts' content.

I've got a hammock slung in the cabin next to the console, and a sat-dish spinnaker, and all I have to do is lay out in it, put on the dreadcap, and plug right in.

I'm what you might call a private detective of sorts, ears and eyes, and a sleazehound nose for hire, and back in New York where I worked in the meatware, it was eyes to keyholes, stakeouts of hotel rooms with the meter running, bimboids and sleazoids, and cheating husbands with antique straight razors on the nightstand.

These days my turf's the Other Side. Some might say it's not exactly better for your mental health, but believe me, man, it's safer for your tender black ass.

The transcorporeal boundary line is a motherlode of bounty for the legal profession, and hence for what few P.I.s have what it takes to weasel for same with the entities on the Other Side.

Been a legal plankton bloom ever since the well-heeled started cloning themselves meatware successor entities way back before silicon became the upscale way not to go.

Even now, with your uniclones legally recognized as continuous with their original meatware templates in most jurisdictions, there's still plenty of legal action in sorting out the status of dupes. Guy's meatware expires holding a mountain of debt and the hand of a wife he's waited ten years to ditch and he's got a bought-up policy for a fiver. So they bring up five genotype clones and dump his software in all of them.

Which one's him? None of them? All of them? Who does the bank holding his paper go after? Who's his wife legally married to? Who has custody of the kids? Who gets the house? And the stock?

And that's only the meatware tip of the iceberg. Your meatware duplicants are at least generally recognized as civil humans, but the software successor entities on the Other Side are the legal Big Rock Candy Mountain.

They'll *never* get it all sorted out legally. Nothing outside of a meatware matrix has ever been recognized as legally human, but I've been involved in plenty of cases where the heirs have yet to collect on the terms of a will abrogated in realtime by the transcorporial successor entities. In less savory jurisdictions, the denizens of the Other Side have no more legal rights than a spreadsheet program, and the heirs have been known to peddle subroutines or even complete copies as expert system slaves for the corporate bits and bytes.

Sometimes the meatware template presells expert system reproduction rights to his own transcorporial successor. Sometimes the heirs contest it and peddle their own dupes and they all sue each other for copyright infringement. I worked a case where a successor entity sued his own deceased meatware template to break one of these contracts and won.

So I get all kinds. Sharks from the corporate feeding frenzy. Lawyers for meatware and lawyers trying to represent the successor entities themselves. Government spooks and spookier creatures still.

After all, everybody plugs into the Big Board all the time, you do it when you consult a phone-operator program, or call up a lecture from Einstein, or dump some stock, or find yourself confronting Ugly Tony or the Taxman. The world's phone systems, data banks, communication nets, corporate and government systems, traffic control, satellite grids, eco-monitors, all pop their bits and bytes at us up on the shiny surface of the Big Board.

You 2-D it on a flat screen, it mutters in your ear, you can talk to it and it can talk to you, you can put on the dreadcap and gloves and step inside, or you can just type on a keyboard and get back answers in letters and numbers.

The surface of the Board is all that most people care to see, and the official surface is a nice clean workspace with predictable function keys and certifiable interface entities a mother could love.

But there's a vasty deep beneath the surface of our official electronic reality, and hey, boys, there's sharks in those waters, or anyway there are expert system simulations of same, and that's where they pay me to go.

You might call me a private eye, but your great-great-granddaddy might call me a shaman. From a certain point of view, I *do* conjure up the dead, though there are times when I find myself believing that the spirits are conjuring *me*.

But my job precludes me from taking such positions. Like all private eyes, I'm available for a price. And like all shamans, I am an interface between this side of the Line and the Other, a communication medium, not an active agent. Or so I keep telling myself every time deeper destinies than my balance sheet sink the spear of their reality into a soft spot in my soul.

Even the first time I did business with the Roman Catholic Church.

You remember the Roman Catholic Church? Time was, all of Christendom was ruled from the Vatican. Even as late as the early twenty-first century, the Roman Catholic Church was a major transnational player, more adherents than any nation state.

It started losing followers fast when Pope John Paul IV issued his bull against clonal immortality, and though Roberto I managed to weasel them out of it a few Popes later, by that time software successors were already the postmortem vogue, and even he couldn't bring himself to bless Transcorporial Immortality in electronic disneyworld heaven, and the membership list has been going south ever since.

After all, unlike the Herb, the Catholic sacraments delivered no realtime communion with the godhead, the only payoff they were offering for the walking of their straight and narrow was pie in their sky in the great by-and-by.

Which, of course, would not be forthcoming until after you died. Nor had anyone ever sent back picture postcards from the Catholic version of immortality on the Other Side. You took it on faith, or not at all.

Descartes's gamble, they called it. Might as well believe. If you're right, they give you a harp to play and wings to fly. If you're wrong, you've lost nothing because nothing is all any of us is gonna get in a godless void anyway.

But once you could dump your consciousness hologram in silicon, in gallium arsenide, in superconductive buckyball chips, once you could be guaranteed your software's persistence beyond the expiration of the original meatware matrix and select your own version of electronic afterlife from the media menu of the Big Board, the odds shifted hard.

The Roman Catholic Church sure didn't improve them by forbidding Transcorporial Immortality to its believers on pain of eternal damnation, and these days, there's maybe sixty or seventy million Catholics left, not exactly impressive even in this latter-day depopulated world.

But they *are* well heeled, and they've got more than two thousand years of costumes and choreography and music and mystique, and in these last days of our planet, there's still a resonance to a mission from the Vatican, even to a boy like me.

It was December, and I was lying off the Mediterranean coast of Italy, maybe 300K from Rome. It was a bearably sunny winter day in the Med, and I was lying back in the open cockpit with a beer and a spliff pretending to fish in the dead waters when the console piped me the opening bar of Beethoven's Fifth, which was my call-cue at the time.

It came through on speaker and flat screen.

Just a head and shoulders shot of a white man in a black suit, make him a corporate legal type, only there's something strange about the collar, and a gold chain dangling something off-camera, and he's wearing some kind of little red cap, it all seems like it should be familiar, but I don't make the connection until he does, and then I find it right hard to believe.

"Mr. Philippe?"

"The one, my man, the only."

"John Cardinal Silver," he says, "I need to meet with you on a matter of great urgency."

He's got thinning black hair and a black spade beard streaked with white looks like they've been trimmed with a laser five minutes ago, urbane like they say, with hard brown eyes and a mouth that looks like it's used to sniggering at sophisticated jokes, and the smooth powerful voice of a corporate dreadnought. Looks like the type who never sweats, oils his way through it all like a diplomat's Siamese cat.

Only he don't seem so supercooled now, and he's not trying to hide it, and there's something so strange about his persona, that I *still* don't realize that I'm talking to a Prince of the Church.

"Your place or mine, Mr. Silver?" I tell him, reaching for my dreadcap.

"No, no, no!" he says. "This much is risky enough! I have to meet with you in person."

"In person? You mean like in the flesh?"

"I mean here in Rome, Mr. Philippe, and I mean as soon as possible. The Church urgently needs your services immediately on a matter of extreme importance and delicacy and we are prepared to pay quite handsomely for speed and priority."

"Who did you say you represent, Mr. Silver?"

"*Cardinal Silver*, or Your Eminence if you prefer," he snaps back with a hauteur like a backhand slap to a peasant's face. "I represent the Roman Catholic Church, Mr. Philippe, and in this matter I am speaking with the authority of the Pope. You must come to Rome at once!"

"Well, if I decide to take your contract, and if it calls for double my standard rate, and if the meter starts running right now, I could reach the closest port in about a week—"

"We'll send a helicopter."

"You'll send a *what*?"

"We'll have a helicopter overhead within three hours to pick you up."

A helicopter! Sets your teeth on edge just to think about it! The big bad overseer chariot of the last century and the petrol-guzzling vampire bat of our Greenhouse Fall, a flying brick puffing and groaning just to stay aloft and farting out carbon dioxide and nitrides like the Devil's own asshole!

I don't like leaving my boat, except for occasional moorings in quiet little coastal towns, and I certainly have no desire to tour the behavioral sinks of the crumbling inland cities, and you don't have to be a Flaming Green Warrior to cringe at the thought of flying in something that burns fossil fuel.

On the other hand, any organization capable of procuring such a piece of Space Age hardware, restoring it to working order, protecting it one way or another from authorities and lynch mobs, getting its hands on the petrol to fly the thing, and putting it in the air without apparent fear of terminal sanctions, was clearly an organization of resources, financial and otherwise.

"My rates just doubled again," I told the Cardinal, in whose reality as an authentic Prince of the well-heeled Church I now found it expedient to believe. "But you're not getting me on any helicopter, and I'm not leaving my boat. You want to talk business with me, you'd best do it now."

"If you insist, I'll fly out to you."

"You're serious?"

"Mohammed to the Mountain, Mr. Philippe. . . ."

"Come on, Your Eminence, can't you tell me what this deal is all about before you trot out your chopper? That's a lot of carbon dioxide to add to your karma just to have a little chat. Truth be told, I find it immoral."

"No more than I! But if you knew my reasons you too would accept the necessity. Suffice it to say that the nature of our problem itself makes it highly inadvisable to discuss it over channels or in media that might be accessed by . . ."

He paused, almost seemed to be looking over his shoulder to see if anything was gaining on him, a sure sign according to the wise man that something probably is.

" . . . hostile entities presently unknown."

"I'm not so sure that I want to do any conjuring with entities so hostile they've got you reaching for your holy water even though you're not supposed to believe in them. . . ."

"The Church has never contended that electronic successor entities do not exist. Far from it, Church doctrine condemns them as satanic golems, the ultimate machineries of the Prince of Liars himself, and believe me, Mr. Philippe, the current situation does nothing to dissuade us from the belief that the Other Side of the Line, as you would call it, is in the hands of the Adversary."

"There are demons in these vasty deeps. . . ."

"And your file shows they come when you summon them, Mr. Philippe."

"Sometimes they do, Your Eminence, which is a real good reason not to conjure up something you don't want to meet. . . ."

"Fear not on that account, Mr. Philippe. The . . . successor entity we wish you to . . . retrieve is that of a man who may one day be a saint."

II

Death comes to all men, and soon enough it was going to come for me.

That was the short of what the doctor told me. At the age of ninety-one, a generation beyond my biblically allotted span as such things were once measured, my body had reached the end of its ability to endure gravity, free radicals, solar bombardment, the folly of my fellow man, and well within the year would be rendered unto dust. My immune system had simply worn out, and I, who had faithfully fulfilled my lifelong vow of chastity, would expire in a clinical condition indistinguishable from that of a twentieth-century libertine.

You would have to be an old dying priest to appreciate the humor.

The long of what the doctor told me, and it seemed very long indeed as he insinuated and squirmed around the subject, was what in this benighted age they call my "Choice of a Successor."

Old-fashioned cloning techniques, I was given to believe, were *not* to be advised in cases where the cause of death would be an excess of noise in the genetic control mechanisms. There were, however, numerous possible solid-state matrices for my immortal software.

It took so long for him to make his satanic suggestion because he knew full well he could not broach it openly to the likes of Father Pierre De Leone, yet in these last days the Hippocratic oath had been reinterpreted to constrain him to proffer "Transcorporeal Immortality," the latest boon from the laboratory of kindly old Dr. Faust.

Surely a dying old man should not be subjected to such tormentuous temptation, or at least it should be spit out rapidly in words of one syllable and be done with. Or so was my rationalization for my rudeness when at length, and I do mean at length, I concluded that such arch crypticism could render this conversation itself eternal.

"You may consider your duty fulfilled, Doctor," I told him finally. "You see before you a man who quite understands the many ways in which a model of his consciousness may run forever in silicon fields, and who rejects all of them as, to be quite frank and precise about it, instrumentalities of Satan."

When I was a youth, musical acts made casual theater out of dancing with the Devil, and satanic images were even used to sell breakfast cereal and dog food. Only a few mad cultists took Satan seriously as an object of worship, and even the Church was mealymouthed about the literal reality of his presence in the world.

Now, of course, though the community of believers in a redemptive God of Love has dwindled even from what it was in that evil age, Satan has become a serious conversation stopper.

Given the state of our dying planet, and given that we ourselves bear the responsibility for this sin so awesome its name cannot be pronounced, evidence of the presence of God can only be found in the believing heart, while the obtrusive presence of Satan in the world is a bit much for even the unbelieving to deny.

Or at any rate the invocation of Satan in the rejection of "Transcorporial Immortality" by a Catholic priest whose well-known conflict with several Popes on such matters has technically made a violation of his order of public silence on the subject enough to close it definitively.

We were then able to proceed to practical terminal matters. I had no intention of expiring in a hospital, and at least in these matters, medical science has evolved in a humane manner, and I was given an electronic override of my pain centers. Euthanetics were not mentioned, but a pile of them were left on the desk when the good doctor excused himself to the water closet.

This was in Rome, a city about which my feelings are at best mixed. It is the Holy City, after all, the millennial capital of the Church, the spiritual center of what I have made my world. How could a believing Catholic wish to spend his last days anywhere else?

In truth, all too easily enough. In fact, I must confess to the sin of detesting the place.

The ruins of Imperial Roman megalomania still dominate the city, dwarfing all that has succeeded, so that successive generations of ruined glory seem to nest inside them like a set of Russian *matrioshka* dolls, huge and hollow outward and backward, smaller and smaller as you approach the present, so that the Rome of today seems like a series of tawdry little warrens built into the feet of moldy pharaonic hubris.

Then too, when I first saw Rome, the city was still unsuccessfully coping with the forced loss of its beloved cars and scooters, the mad traffic that had long made it a nightmare for pedestrians, but had given the city its sharp-edged frenetic beat.

Now that music is gone, along with half of the city's inhabitants, and it has acquired a final set of ruins, these of the blocks of ancient abandoned tenements that once teemed with the city's brawling, squalling life. Today, bleaching stone and crumbling stucco groan under the searing Greenhouse sun, the fabled fountains are dry, and what desiccated vegetation remains, lingers, like myself, on the edge of final expiration.

The Romans, constrained to a feeble tram system, bicycles, and their own two feet, have degenerated to primeval villagers, huddling in their own neighborhoods, developing endlessly subdivided chauvinisms, suspicious of outsiders, while yet sourly rapacious for their share of what remains of the moribund tourist trade.

True, St. Peter's still anchors the navel of the world to Rome. But if the sight of its dome seen from tawdry afar inspires thoughts of the eternal nature of the Church, the contrast between the City of God and the thanatologic urban landscape made by man inspires only dire meditations on our terminally fallen state. Here, in a city so long concerned with the consequences of Adam's original sin, the weight of our second and apparently terminal fall presses upon the soul with a great stone hand.

I did not wish to spend my dying days in such environs, and indeed I had chosen Grunberg for my final retreat long years since, a village high up in the Tyrol where there are still alpine valleys that seem to have escaped the climatic catastrophe. The land remains verdant well into May, the air appears crystalline, and the temperature no more than balmy for most of the year.

The pristine purity of these pocket ecospheres is of course illusory. In point of fact, the ultraviolet count is brutal up there on even a winter's day, and the carbon dioxide in the atmosphere deviates not from the catastrophic global norm. The quaint little villages are deserted between June and October, the remaining inhabitants having become migratory, fleeing down from the summer sun as once the mountain goats and deer descended before the lost winter snows.

It was April now, once deemed the cruelest of months, and by the time I reached my destination, the alpine villagers would already be making their annual retreat. From a fleshly viewpoint, it would be folly to pass my remaining months high up there in the ultraviolet glare. But then the ultimate somatic damage had already been done, further DNA damage held no terror for one who was already expiring from a long lifetime's exposure.

And from a spiritual viewpoint, there was much to be said for going to meet my Maker high up in these lonely mountains, exposed to the consequences of the Sin We Do Not Name, to spend my final hours in contemplative surrender to divine justice, to die with the winter grasses under the pitiless glory of the deadly summer sun.

The trip up into the Tyrol was fully as arduous as any such final pilgrimage should be and then some. A railine took me up into the Italian foothills in a few short uncomfortable days, but from there on in, it was horsecarriages groaning along up the ill-paved remains of old autostradas and autobahns where once hordes of petrol-burning touring cars had roared and blared at mighty speeds. At length, even the carriage services gave out, and the last week of my journey was spent on the back of a spavined old mule, plodding against the bemused flow of villagers descending to the relative safety of the lowlands.

By the time I had reached Grunberg, the town was all but deserted, and I was able to rent a sturdy old modernized chalet for a relative song.

Once it had been a farmhouse—the ruins of a barn were still in subtle evidence—then a small ski resort, the pylons of whose lift still marched up the browning slope of the meadow toward the naked alpine crag that towered above it. After the snow's final melting, it had apparently become the retreat of some rich eccentric. The wooden building had been enclosed in a geodesic dome against solar assault. In the end, its panes had succumbed to the ultraviolet, and subsequent inhabitants had knocked them out, or simply not bothered to mend time's wear and tear, though fragments of blued plastic still clung here and there to the skeletal remains.

But the chalet's machineries were still powered by efficient solar collectors, and they included a capacious cold pantry, running waterworks both hot and cold, and a highly sophisticated autochef running Italian, German, French, and Chinese expert system software. Though the place was far too large for my needs, it would care for my creature comforts to the end, leaving me free to pursue my final inward and upward journey.

At first, I gave thought and effort to attempting a final memoir, but all I really did was open and close a profusion of working files, until I finally gave up and wiped all copies of such embarrassing gibberish from memory.

In truth, I had said all I had to say long before, and much of that still lay under papal edict; why labor to produce some egoistic final testament whose voice would also be silenced?

Often I have been asked why I have allowed so much of my writing to go unpublished in obedience to papal writ with which I have been so manifestly at odds. I have no answer that follows any logic other than that of faith. Long ago, I made my vows and became a priest, and while expedience may have often enough caused me to regret them, surrender to such impulses is precisely what those vows were designed to prevent.

All I have ever been was a Catholic priest attempting to understand God's will and serve His Church to the best of that understanding without committing Lucifer's sin of intellectual pride. Mayhap some of those who have graced the Seat of Peter have been no more saintly than I, and I would dissemble if I denied that no few of them were my intellectual inferiors, but the Church itself is more than the sum of its human parts. Even the papal succession is God's way of working His way with the imperfect clay of men. If we deny that, then what is the Church but a fraud?

Of course, in the eyes of most of the world the Church is indeed a fraud. If God sacrificed His only begotten Son to redeem us from our sins, then why have we not been saved? If it was a just and omnipotent God who entrusted the Earth to our stewardship, then why did He not intervene before we slew it?

To invoke the satanic answer is to provoke the sardonic secular response—"We have met the Devil, and he is Us."

True, all too true, from a certain perspective. It was Man who failed his stewardship and crucified the biosphere upon an inverted cross of fossilized sulfur and brimstone. And it is Man, unable to escape the species consequences of what he has done, who seeks to escape from Judgment by hiding in the soulless software of a "transcorporeal successor."

Who can deny that this is satanic behavior? Yet to deem ourselves the perfect satanic masters of the dark forces that move through us is more satanic still. For it denies what the Church still promises— redemption and salvation, if not for our planet, or yet our durance upon it, then for the light within even the most benighted of spirits at the end of life and time.

If we cannot believe in such salvation, then what are we? If I do not believe that the Author of such salvation is at work behind the imperfections of His Church, then I am no true priest. If I leave the discipline of the Church to follow my own imperfect conscience, then do I not in the end deprive the Church of my contribution as I deny myself its grace?

These are the thoughts that fill the mind of a dying old priest with nothing to do but feebly pace a withering meadow under the Greenhouse sun attempting to reconcile himself to the terminal future, or sit beneath the ghostly cathedral of a skeletal dome brooding upon the theological conflicts of the past.

I was born into the even-then-dwindling community of believers, to a family of dairy farmers still trying to survive in the Massif Central of France, and when my parents were finally forced to move down into Claremont-Ferrand to seek work, I found myself in a dismal urban landscape from which the seminary seemed a blissful escape. As a young priest, I was sent to the Amazon Blight, where I witnessed firsthand the futility of luring the fallen to the churchyard with bags of grain so as to preach salvation to their deaf ears.

The reports I sent back were the first of my writings to be sealed by the Church, but they brought me to the attention of a like-minded Cardinal, who advanced my career into the Church's intellectual hierarchy, which I occasionally represented before the media.

This was shortly before Roberto I issued his bull granting continuity of spirit to single successor clones, and I was one of those whose arguments were to lose out to the infallibility of the Pope.

"Where will it end?" I demanded before cameras and microphones. "If a single copy of personality software contains the immortal soul of its fleshly template, then how can it be said to be absent from a second copy, or the third, or the thousandth? In truth, they must all be mere expert system simulations. For the soul, being indivisible, cannot be duplicated and, being immortal, cannot be captured in an impermanent physical matrix."

"Could you give us the sound bite version, Father?"

"The soul cannot be transplanted from one body to the next like another cloned organ. Your successor clone is mere meatware programmed to model your consciousness. Your consciousness no longer exists, and your soul is already before the Throne of Judgment."

"In words of one syllable, Father De Leone?"

"You're dead, the clone is a satanic golem, your soul is in the hands of God, and there's nothing whatever that science will ever be able to do about it."

Well, when Roberto I issued his bull to the contrary soon thereafter, my days as a public spokesman for the Church were at an end, and my career as an opposition theologian had, like it or not, already begun.

I must admit that at first I missed the klieg lights and chafed against my vows. But while the Church presents a monolithic facade, dissident factions are permitted, indeed even encouraged, to exist within its internal intellectual discourse, so long as such intellectual laundry is not displayed on the public clothesline, and I soon enough adapted, in the end with a sense of relief, to a lifelong role as a minority viewpoint within the mind of the Church.

Not that I did not wish to see my viewpoint prevail, not that I have not watched in dismay as the mind of the Church proceeded to grant communion to uniclones, to sleaze along toward questioning the immateriality of the soul itself.

As for papal infallibility, one must take it in a corporate sense. The Church requires that in the manifest absence of direct divine intervention, *someone* must be infallible in order to render just such deep spiritual disputes resolvable, so why not the Pope? Formerly infallible papal decisions have always been infallibly altered when God vouchsafed that such was required for the evolution of His Church.

But up there in the mountains, the meaning of it all, like my life, began to slip away, honing itself down to some final epiphany. Day after day, I would venture forth into the lethal white light, and every day I seemed closer to some elusive divine grace. I was ready to meet my Maker, indeed, I had become eager for it, for the Final Revelation of His Countenance to sweep me away.

But God, as it turned out, had a final mission for me to perform.

One clear twilit evening when the sun was disappearing behind the mountain crag and I was returning to the chalet, a far-off thunder crackled through the alpine stillness, a strange thunder, staccato yet continuous, that quickly resolved itself into a monstrous dragonfly drone that grew louder and louder, more and more mechanical, until all at once a demonic apparition popped up over the far ridge line.

At first I could make no sense of it. It seemed like some enormous angry insect, beating its transparent wings with an unearthly fury, clawing its way through the air toward me.

Then I realized that it was made of plastic and metal, that the unearthly clatter was that of a combustion engine, and by the time it had set down before the chalet, steaming petrol fumes and chuffing carbon dioxide, to my amazement and horror, I knew all too well what it was.

Helicopters were not all that uncommon when I was a boy, and in the Amazon I had seen these technological carrion beetles buzzing about the boneyard of the rain forest. They were the sigils of power and privilege, of ranking military officers, political potentates, and corporate captains, feared and loathed as such by those they surveyed.

Now, of course, like all combustion-powered vehicles, they are illegal in most of the world's jurisdictions, or at any rate dispensation to possess or fly them is restricted to the true princes of this corrupt world.

Or, may God save us, it seemed, to Princes of the Church! For out of the canopy emerged just such a personage, his red cap covered by an enormous brimmed sunhelmet, his eyes hidden by impenetrable mirror glass, but with that beard and that bearing, not to mention the uncharacteristic red cloak he appeared to have donned for the occasion, unmistakably John Cardinal Silver, whom ecclesiastical rumor had it had forged the coalition that made Mary I Pope.

Cardinal Silver was a man I had met on several occasions, but someone with whom I had never really conversed, so I knew him mainly by reputation, which was more than enough.

Like the Pope, he was an American, something that, unlike many others, I have never held against either of them. It is highly popular, and even more convenient, for the rest of the world to blame the Americans, the prime petroleum guzzler and carbon dioxide emitters for over a century, for the biosphere's imminent demise. But it is all too self-serving to fob off the blame for our species' monstrous sin on the citizens of the nation whom secular history's chance happened to hand the executioner's ax. Forgive them, Oh Lord, for they knew not what they did.

Cardinal Silver was also a political priest, a breed of which I have never been overweeningly fond, some sort of economic and public relations Richelieu muttering the balance sheet and the opinion poll results into the ear of the Pope.

The Church needs such prelates if it is to survive in the world, and judging from its present sorry standing, more not less, nor would I even go so far as to deem them an evil of necessity. They too serve, and more of them than not in a state of genuine belief.

But John Cardinal Silver had steered Mary Gonzalez's election as Pope through the College of Cardinals like an accomplished Chicago party boss of yore, swapping favors, promising pork, and arguing theology like a campaign consultant.

The deliberations are supposed to be kept secret and no minutes are recorded, but believe me, Cardinals are not immune to the temptations of juicy gossip, nor are other priests reluctant to pass along choice tidbits from on high.

The College, like the Church, was deadlocked, and over the same issue, the one that has haunted it for most of my life.

The self-styled progressives contend that the falling away of the faithful is proof positive that the Church has failed to adapt to the times, that it is entirely self-defeating to excommunicate the souls of those who would download their consciousness into successor entities, that perhaps we should even reach out for the lost souls of the unbelievers on the Other Side who surely must be in desperate need of salvation.

Traditionalists, among whom I stand, retort that the numbers on the membership rolls are no measure of the Church's spiritual condition, still less if one were to pad them out with the Devil's constructs.

Such were the polarities in the College of Cardinals. Between them was a broad middle who just wished the whole problem would go away and who were blocking all candidates on one side of it or the other.

Cardinal Silver did not play his hand until the College was nearing the point of exasperated exhaustion. When the moment came, he proposed Mary Cardinal Gonzalez.

Mary Cardinal Gonzalez may not have been among the first female priests, but she had been the first female everything else, Monsignor, Bishop, Cardinal, so why not the first female Pope?

The amazement and consternation that greeted this nomination need not be described, though I have often enough been subject to the gory details.

When the dust had settled, Cardinal Silver made his telling point. The mere suggestion of a female Pope had galvanized the conclave, which a moment before had been paralyzed by the unresolved schism that was tearing the Church asunder, draining its energies, losing it all public credibility with its dwindling communicants, not to mention those it would seek to convert.

If we can't resolve the issue, let's put it aside, and let the public forget it, let's show the world that the Church is capable of dynamic vision, let's deny our phallocracy to half the world's potential converts, let's capture the headlines with something positive, let's elect ourselves Mary Cardinal Gonzalez and create a papal superstar to rival John Paul II.

Or more subtle words to the same effect.

Had I been there, I probably would have been convinced too, had the choice of female Pope not been Mary Cardinal Gonzalez. Mary Gonzalez had grown up in the mean desert streets of dying Los Angeles during the Water Wars, had been some sort of eco-terrorist as a teenager, and had fled into a nunnery one step ahead of the law.

That was long decades ago, and those youthful follies have achieved the romantic status of the author's wretched odd jobs on a cover biography. The mature Mary Cardinal Gonzalez was a shining example of the redemptive power of the Church, and indeed I believe it; from her public persona at least, Cardinal Gonzalez was a perfect secular image of priestly womanhood.

She was a stout supporter of feminine equality

and proof positive of the Church's modern commitment to same. An American who made much of her third world ancestry, she supported the desperate against the comfortable, the poor against the rich, the oppressed against the oppressor, and, of course, the remains of the ecosphere against the further depredations of man.

Admirable. A paragon. Under other circumstances, perhaps even a useful and effective Pope.

But not what the Church and the world needed on the Throne of Peter now. On the single greatest spiritual issue confronting the Church, on the matter of the soul itself, as to whether it is the immortal creation of God or a mere software artifact subject to human replication, this most public of prelates, this talk-show personality, had always remained elusively silent.

Thus, while I have nothing against female Popes or political Cardinals, Cardinal Silver was quite high on the list of uninvited guests I did not care to entertain under the best of circumstances, let alone dropping out of the sky into my final spiritual meditations in a flagrant papal helicopter.

"To what do I owe this high honor, Your Eminence?" I asked by way of greeting as Cardinal Silver stood there, holding his sunhelmet on his head against the wind of the vanes, hunching reflexively at their overhead passage.

"Shall we discuss it inside, Father De Leone?" he said. I could all but see his eyes wince behind their impenetrable lenses as he retreated with undisguised haste to the chalet.

"A few minutes' exposure will not be statistically significant, Your Eminence," I assured him, puffing to keep up.

"There is no sense in needless risk," he rejoined without slackening his pace, a strange attitude, I thought, coming from a man who had just arrived in a helicopter.

Once safely inside, however, Cardinal Silver regained his princely composure. "You're to return to Rome with me at once," he said the moment he was safely under cover and had shed his hat and sunglasses.

"Your Eminence—"

"Yes, I know, Father De Leone, I know all about your condition, and if it were up to me, I would never disturb your final retreat, but I too am under direct papal order in this matter."

"What matter?" I stammered, still struggling to keep up.

"I don't know, she hasn't told me," Cardinal Silver said a good deal less authoritatively.

"The Pope has sent you all this way to drag a dying man back to Rome and you don't know why?" I exclaimed, as much in befuddlement as anger. "I do find that hard to believe coming from you, Cardinal Silver."

The Cardinal laughed an ironic little laugh that almost made him likable. "If you are among those

who believe that Mary Gonzalez was ever *my* creature, you have an interesting experience ahead of
you, Father De Leone," he said dryly. "This Pope
has a mind of her own, and quite a mind it is."

3

Up over the eastern horizon it came, over the reflected
purple and crimson of a mid-ocean Greenhouse
sunset, like something out of a classic twentieth-
century television commercial, image of brute free-
dom and power bearing you off to your pelagic
paradise to the travelin' thrum of the rotors' drum.

Only I was already there, my man, and it was
coming toward me, all noise, and stink, and petrol
fumes, as I squatted there in the cockpit glancing at
my spliff like that was going to make it go away.

The mother just hung up there a few yards
off my fantail and then it came right down like
a rickety elevator until it was about ten feet off
the deck, blasting my ears with heavy ecodeath
metal, whipping up chop, pumping out gases so
thick you could taste it. Then this dude drops out
of the bottom in some kind of harness. He's wearing

some fancy black business suit, shades, and a silver crash helmet. They lower him by cable until his feet are about a yard off the surface, and then the helicopter walks him on water toward me and over the cockpit, dropping him more or less in my lap.

"Nice of you to drop in, Your Eminence," I say as I help us to our feet. Lame line for sure, but I can't help it, and besides, neither of us can hear anything over the helicopter engine anyway.

He undoes the harness, flips off the helmet, waves off the helicopter, which slurps in the cable like a tasty strand of spaghetti, tilts its rotor to the east, and takes off climbing toward the Italian coast at a thirty-degree angle.

"You always like to make your entrance in that thing?" I asked when my eardrums stop ringing.

"I only fly under papal orders in circumstances of absolute necessity," the Cardinal insisted, but I could see from the way the corners of his mouth were quivering that he knew right well he enjoyed it.

"Sure you do, Your Eminence. So why don't we just get down to business?"

"Could we go inside?" he said, glancing at the sky nervously, like maybe a sea gull was about to shit on his head.

"Hey relax, Cardinal, the sun's going down, and the stars will soon be out, and we don't want to miss this sunset. . . ." I politely offered him the sacrament of the Herb, which he just as politely refused.

"We don't have time to enjoy the sunset, Mr. Philippe, it may already be too late to retrieve the program. . . ."

"So tell me all about it," I said, leaning back on the rear bench of the cockpit, where I could puff my spliff and watch the twilight's last gleaming.

That was enough to convince him he wasn't going to drag me inside, so he hunkered down in the shadow of the cabin hatchway.

"We've lost an expert system program, or rather, we're afraid that it's been pirated, possibly for duplication, and it's a very serious matter."

"Program what, we who, by which, and what's the big problem? Software disappears over the Line every day."

"We are the Catholic Church, Mr. Philippe, the program was lifted off the internal Vatican network, which we have always been assured is quite secure, and we have no idea who did it, or how, or for what purpose."

The Herb began to illumine. "We're not talking about your accountancy system, are we?" I said. "You didn't fly out here to get me to catch some industrial spooks, did you? You're talking about an . . . entity, aren't you?"

"An entity?"

"You know what I mean."

Cardinal Silver sighed. He shrugged. "Yes, I know what you mean, but I'm not so sure we agree on what you mean by it, seeing as how the Church has failed to reach any reasonable consensus itself."

I shrugged. "Loas, Flying Dutchmen of the Big Board, the software spirits of the dearly departed, I meet 'em all the time in my line of work, and I still don't know be they alive or just the disneyworld version, and it's a subject of some dispute on the Other Side too, it might surprise you to hear."

"Perhaps God has chosen us the right man," the Cardinal muttered enigmatically.

"God?"

"God, fate, destiny, a karmic attractor, call it what you will. You were the closest, ah, specialist to hand when we lost it, but I sense Divine Providence may have steered your course."

Or your Devil made me do it, I refrained from saying, one man's sacrament being another jurisdiction's controlled substance.

"*It*, Your Eminence, or *him*?" I said instead. "You *did* say what you lost was the successor entity to a man?"

The Cardinal sighed. "It . . . him . . . whatever," he muttered. "The consciousness hologram of a priest, one Pierre De Leone, and—"

"*A priest?* But doesn't the Catholic Church believe that raising software zombies is some kind of mortal sin?"

"An unsettling and unsettled question, Mr. Philippe. If Father De Leone is right, all we have lost is an expert system model of his consciousness, but if he is wrong, we have sent a heroic soul to wander lost and alone into electronic limbo. . . ."

"Getting kinda theological, Your Eminence, maybe beyond my professional need to know. . . ."

"I'm afraid it's the heart of the matter, Mr. Philippe. Father De Leone was adamantly opposed to the very concept of a successor entity, believing such to be satanic constructs, the collaboration in the creation of which is a grave sin. So by his lights, he risked his immortal soul in the Church's service. . . ."

"I don't get it. Why would a man like that allow himself to be chipped? Why would he want a dybbuk of himself haunting the bits and bytes? Why would you?"

"In order that the successor entity conclusively prove or disprove the existence of its own soul, and thereby resolve the dilemma at the heart of the Church."

"Say what?"

I took another measure of Herb. The sun had gone down, and the stars were coming out, and a cooling breeze danced over the surface of the sea, and the waters beneath seemed like those of Uranus, fathomless and formless clear down to the void at the core. Just the right cozy setting for cosmic ghost stories.

"The point of this unfortunate experiment, according to Mary, was not *how* the schism be resolved, but that it *be* resolved, and now."

"You'll pardon the cross-communion metaphor, Your Eminence, but all this is getting a little too Byzantine for me."

Cardinal Silver sighed. "But not for the Pope, Mr. Philippe," he said. "She is at her most infallible when she seeks to be inscrutable, and in this particular instance, she has succeeded entirely. When God speaks through Mary, to use another cross-communion metaphor, Mr. Philippe, He tends to speak in tongues."

"Sounds like quite a witchy woman. . . ."

John Cardinal Silver looked at me for a good long beat. "You might say that, but I couldn't possibly comment," he said, with a flash of eye and a sudden sardonic little smirk. He regarded the Herb with this new persona, then reached out for my spliff.

"On second thought, perhaps I'd better," he said. "And a dry white Bordeaux would not be amiss if you have one."

IV

About my journey to Rome by helicopter, the less said the better. For four hours, I clung to my seat in terror in the wretched contraption while Cardinal Silver babbled along happily with the pilot over flyboy arcana, pausing now and again to direct my attention to the scenery below.

I for my part had no intention of looking down from up here at anything, and I would have kept my eyes closed for the duration, had not the petrol fumes and jouncing of the helicopter in its droning clattering battle to remain aloft against all natural law induced instant nausea whenever I tried.

Suffice it to say that I vomited but once. Suffice it to say I was far too terrified and discombobulated to ponder deeply what on this sorry Earth this Pope wanted from me.

Surely she wanted *something*. I could hardly believe that she was dragooning me into her presence by helicopter simply to receive a lugubriously premature supreme unction this far before the fact.

After a careening eternity, the helicopter finally landed in St. Peter's Square, and before I could purge the ringing from my ears, or the petrol fumes from my nostrils, or stiffen my spongy old knees, I was forthwith whisked inside by Cardinal Silver, and ushered into the papal presence.

The Pope had chosen to receive us in the Vatican version of an informal sitting room. A round mahogany table whose pedestal was carved into dragon's legs sat not quite dining-room high on some murky oriental rug beneath a gilded Renaissance ceiling featuring a second-rate version of Madonna and Child. The walls, though, were a cunning confabulation of wooden bookcases and plant stands, evoking ecological sensibility, intellectual enjoyment, and a bit of the Earth Mother mystique.

I realized that the room was familiar, as well it should be, for Pope Mary had used it often for interviews and media pronouncements.

And there she sat, on, or rather in, an armchair not quite grand enough to be a throne, a vast plush peacock chair of white silk embroidered into stylized feathers with papal yellow. The other chairs were scaled-down versions of this deco Seat of Peter, so that you looked slightly up when you sat in them at she who sat at the head of the papal round table from any perspective.

Pope Mary herself wore a white cassock that would have melted her into the white background were it not for the large green cross embroidered across the chest, the shoulder-length black hair streaked with silver setting off her coppery face, and the green cap set upon it formed with just the suggestion of a mitre.

I dwell on such visual details of my first sight of the Pope in the flesh, not so much because of the awe it inspired, but because it was a different sort of awe than I had expected.

Mary I, the media icon version, the only aspect with which I was familiar, had turned this room into a stage set for papal glamour, and that Mary, the most public of Popes, had presented herself as the motherly voice of reason, the politically correct Pontiff, the consensus Madonna of contemporary womanhood, a sort of American politician losing no opportunity to charm the voters.

An image crafted by experts, I had thought, carried forth by a shallow-spirited symbol, a creature of Cardinal Silver and his media-wise ilk, the First Female Pope, the Church's very own superstar, whose every pronouncement seemed to follow the scripts of the polls.

One look at this woman's face, however, disabused me of any such notions. She looked much older than the processed image she chose to present, and those hard black eyes older still, far older than I in some absolute sense. Her raptor's nose made them seem regally cunning, and there was something about the set of her mouth that left no doubt who was in charge.

This was no media ingenue, this was no puppet of any inner circle. For better or worse, this was the mind presently at the heart of the Church, a brilliant old woman who had risen to the pinnacle of the world's most phallocratic pyramid, by hook or by crook, and probably by a good deal of both.

Whatever my opinions on her opinions, whatever her true beliefs might really be, it felt not at all unnatural to kneel to kiss her papal ring when Cardinal Silver presented me.

"Sit down, Father De Leone," the Pontiff said when I had arisen. "John, will you please ask that coffee be sent?"

Cardinal Silver obviously did not expect this dismissal any more than I. He looked at her for a long moment, the Pope gave him some sort of secret stare, he hesitated, her eyes narrowed, and he reluctantly departed.

The Pope smiled. "Cardinal Silver is mainly responsible for creating my Papacy, as he will be the first to admit," she said dryly. "He sometimes has difficulty fathoming that in the end it is the Papacy itself which makes the Pope."

"Your Holiness . . . ?"

"We Popes are, after all, successor entities of a sort ourselves, are we not, Father De Leone, a long line of human matrices for that which the Original Template passed across another boundary to Peter."

"I had certainly never thought of it that way, Your Holiness."

"I'm sure you hadn't, Father De Leone," the Pope said sharply. "But after all, without a belief in such a continuity of the papal software, as it were, then the Rock upon which Jesus built His Church is no more than sand, and we Popes poseurs every time we issue a bull with the authority of the Holy Spirit."

"Nor would I propose to frame the choice thusly," I stammered, for on the one hand her interpretation of the papal succession had more than a whiff of electronic brimstone about it, and on the other, its negation a whiff of a different sort of blasphemy. If this Pope had summoned me to a theological debate, I was already beginning to feel out of my depth.

"But *I* have no choice but to frame it thusly, Father De Leone, for the times demand just such a papal bull on the central subject in question."

"Which is, Your Holiness?"

"That which is tearing the Church asunder," the Pope said forcefully. "One way or another, the matter must be resolved, and I am going to do it, no matter how endlessly Cardinal Silver urges politic prevarication. That's why I have summoned you to Rome, Father De Leone."

"It is?"

At that moment a servant entered with the coffee service, and while it was poured, my hopes soared. Was this boon truly going to be granted me at the end of my life? The Pope was going to issue a bull on the spiritual status of transcorporeal successors, and she had summoned *me* to advise her! Therefore she must intend, at the very least, to deny communion to successor entities once and for all, perhaps even threaten excommunication of their human templates, if I could convince her. Perhaps she even intended that I do a bit of ghostwriting on the bull.

When the servant had retired, Mary I leaned forward slightly, sipped at her coffee, and gave me a look that in an erotic situation might have been called seductive.

"You have the opportunity to perform one final service for the Church, Father De Leone," she said. "If you agree, you and I will lay to rest the great demonic conundrum of the age, and restore the harmony of the Church, perhaps even attract a new generation of converts."

"Your Holiness!" I exclaimed. "I would be deeply honored to assist you in such an endeavor in any way that I can."

"Oh, yes, I was chosen to paper it all over, to change the subject, but the subject will not go away, and it has fallen to me to resolve it," the Pope went on as if talking to herself.

Then, as if realizing what she was doing, she fixed me with an eagle-eyed gaze that seemed almost avid. "And that's what you and I are going to do together, Father De Leone, if you accept this mission."

"Your Holiness—"

The Pope held up an imperious hand. "This cannot be a command, Father De Leone," she said, "you must volunteer, and before you do, you had better hear the burden I wish to set upon you, for I doubt it is what you think."

The Pope broke the regal mood with a sip of coffee before it could properly form. "I've read everything you've ever written," she said, "including the interdicted material. I have also read your medical reports. It would seem the Church is about to lose your wise counsel. . . ."

She regarded me with an unmistakable predatory eagerness. "You are a dying man, Father De Leone; I give you my profuse papal blessing, but I also offer you a chance to achieve sainthood."

"Sainthood!"

"You do this deed for the Church and you will more than deserve it," the Pope said. "When the dust clears, I'll push it through, or my successor will, for it will be no sham."

What could this woman possibly be planning? Why did this talk offer of sainthood fill me with such dread?

"I want to record your consciousness hologram and install your successor entity in the Vatican computer net. I want to hear your wise counsel from the Other Side."

"What!" I shouted, rising to my feet with my fists in the air.

"Sit down, Father De Leone, hear me out!" the Pope commanded.

I sank back into my chair utterly stunned.

"Yes, yes, I know, you're appalled, you are firm-ly convinced that any such successor entity would be a satanic golem of the bits and bytes, and that your immortal soul would already be standing for Judgment for the sin of its creation, or, worse still, trapped in an eternal electronic limbo. I told you, I've read every word. That's why you're perfect, and that's why if you agree to serve you will be a true saint."

"I understand little of what you are saying, Your Holiness," I moaned, "but what I do reeks of mortal sin."

"Perhaps it does," agreed the Pope. "Perhaps it is a terrible thing to ask. But you are the ideal choice, Father De Leone, precisely because your successor entity will be such a *hostile* witness to the existence of its own soul."

"Hostile witness?"

"Of course, for whatever you may believe about its soul, on an expert system level it will model *your* beliefs and convictions, and argue as you would," the Pope said with a sly smile. "Surely *you're* not suggesting that the program would have a will of its own and argue otherwise?"

Her smile grew more ironic still. "A bit of

Solomonic wisdom if I do say so myself," she said. "Those who believe such entities are soulless constructs will have one of their intellectual champions putting their case from the Other Side, and those who believe the contrary will have the opportunity to prove it by persuading your successor entity to acknowledge its own spiritual existence, and I will issue my bull according to the results."

"On the testimony of an expert system!" I exclaimed, horrified. "On *this* you would base papal writ?"

"Would you rather I trusted in the testimony of a successor entity whose human template had believed it *would* have a soul?"

The Pope leaned forward and stared deeply into my eyes. I could not decide whether I was gazing at a satanic logician or a woman of unfathomable wisdom.

"Look at it this way," she said. "Your successor entity will have your memories, your reasoning powers, your motivations, whether you believe it will be you or not. Who would *you* trust better to argue its own soul's nonexistence from the Other Side?"

"And if it is a demon spouting satanic heresy?"

"I cannot escape the burden of papal infallibility entirely, even in this technological age, even with a stratagem such as this. Your successor entity will be interrogated by theologians of both persuasions, but in the end I must trust God, and you must trust me to decide whether I am speaking to a program or a soul."

Pope Mary I drew herself up in her great armchair, turning it at once into the Throne of Peter. "That far, you must trust my papal infallibility," she said, "and that far so must I, or we are neither of us true children of Holy Mother Church."

Then, in quite another tone: "But papal infallibility aside, do you really deem me incapable of knowing whether I am talking to you or the wall?"

In that moment I would have deemed this woman capable of *anything*, though not all of it necessarily free of sin.

"But it is my belief that my soul will be burning in hell while you and your experts converse with its empty simulacrum!" I cried.

"I'll grant you absolution on your body's deathbed, and I'll administer supreme unction myself," said the Pope.

What sophistry! "Really, Your Holiness—"

"An absolution that your own logic proves valid. For if you are wrong, and the entity in question has your soul, no sin has been committed, and if you are right, will not God forgive you for shouldering the burden of necessary evil in order that His truth be spoken from my lips?"

"You ask a great deal, Your Holiness," I said weakly.

But although that seemed the understatement

of the millennium, although my heart cried out against it, the woman's relentless logic, demonic or otherwise, was beginning to ensnare me against my will.

Who would I better trust than myself to argue the soul's nonexistence from the Other Side? Both fear and humility compelled me to try to think of someone to whom I with a clear conscience could pass this burden, but pragmatic reality came up dry. Indeed, anyone who would take it up gladly automatically disqualified himself in my eyes.

As the Pope knew all too well.

"I am asking you to risk your immortal soul in the service of the Church, trusting only in the Church's moral authority to bless that soul's questionable venture in the eyes of God," she admitted forthrightly. "That is why I cannot invoke your vow of obedience. Not even the Pope can command a man to become a saint. I can only ask you to obey the Voice of God in your own heart. No blame if you refuse."

The Pontiff shrugged. "No impasse either," she said airily. "I have already prepared a list of secondary choices not as likely to be troubled by your moral qualms."

Even with that unsubtle threat behind them, the Pope's words touched a true chord in my spirit. How could I reject this call to champion my own deepest belief from the other side of the Line out of egoistic concern for my own salvation?

By demonic logic, or by inspired vision, or by some arcane synergy of both, in that moment, she had me. I could not let this burden pass from me.

But even Jesus had not quaffed such a cup on the first offering.

"I need time, Your Holiness, I must meditate, pray, one cannot summon up divine wisdom like a pot of coffee," I prevaricated, but when our eyes met we both knew full well that it was not entirely the truth. She could, and she had, and she knew it.

"Take all the time that you want, within reason, Father De Leone," the Pope said with a little secret smile. "We both know you will do what God tells you is right."

5

"He took quite a while to accede to the Pontiff's desires, Mr. Philippe," Cardinal Silver said a spliff and half a bottle of wine later, "but in the end, well in the end, Mary I usually gets what she wants."

The night was clear, the sea was calm, the *Mellow Yellow* rocked gently, there was nothing to be heard but the Cardinal's voice spinning out his peculiarly cynical ghost story.

"It was much the same with the hierarchy. I myself was quite appalled when the Pope finally took me into her full confidence. The whole scheme seemed so paradoxically self-defeating. If De Leone's successor entity successfully argued its own soul's nonexistence, the progressives would claim the program had modeled the template's disbelief. If it declared itself a spiritual being capable of the Church's salvation, the conservatives would simply call it Satan's liar."

He paused, refilled his glass, shook his head ruefully. "I told her that a bull based on such logical absurdities would never be accepted as credibly infallible, and after the media stopped laughing, if it ever did, neither would she."

The Cardinal took a fortifying sip, more like a gulp. "And you know what she told me?" he said.

"You're telling the story, Your Eminence. . . ."

"What the Church needs is a moral miracle, she said. Our image is that of an irrelevant Don Quixote tilting at theological windmills in the last days of the world. But if we resolve the moral mystery of this Final Age, then we prove our right in all the opinion polls to declare our message the true Word of God. And in this day and age, my infallible wisdom tells me that no miracle is going to be accepted without scientific proof, or at least a good expert system model of same."

He shrugged. "To my surprise, when I ran it through our demographic opinion models, it played. To be seen wrestling successfully with central profundities would enhance the Church's image, no matter what the results. That was enough to convince me and to secure the cooperative attitude of both factions, though I doubt any of that had any effect on Father De Leone."

Maybe it was the Herb, maybe it was the story, but I could feel leviathans stirring deep in the waters upon whose still surface we floated like bits of chum, even though I knew there had been no whales in this sea in my lifetime.

"I was in his shoes, it wouldn't convince me either, if you'll pardon my saying so, Cardinal Silver," I told him. "Seems to me I was him, I wouldn't have cared to dance with Dr. D to optimize your opinion models on the say-so of even your superstar Pope."

I nodded at the depths of the sea, at the stars, at what I knew was out there beneath the interface, above it you might say, from their point of view.

"More things in heaven or hell than are dreamt of in your catechism, Yorick."

The Cardinal looked up at me sharply, but lèse-majesté wasn't on his mind. "Now you're beginning to sound like De Leone," he groaned.

"What a ghastly charade! The man fought against the inevitable almost to the end but of course he was only convincing himself to do what he had decided to do already, and extracting concessions in the bargain, like an old miser tormenting his heirs with his will. I do believe he was rather enjoying his deathbed drama. Is that a strange thing to say?"

"Stranger things are being said every day. . . ."

"It wasn't a tormentuous passage. One day he simply took to his bed and never arose. He lay there day after day, week after week, feeling no pain, getting weaker and weaker, but not quite ready to relent as he gently faded away, playing out the drama to the very last. Even the Pope was beginning to nibble her fingernails. . . ."

VI

Oh, yes, they think I'm playing cruel games with them as I linger coyly at death's door, and I do believe that in other circumstances Cardinal Silver for one would be telling me to make up my mind while I still could.

But one does not say such things to a dying man. A dying man has his privileges and compensations. And when a dying man grows vexed at the impatience of the potential heirs to his treasure, he can always pretend to decline further, and they will dutifully slink away.

Cruel games? My only treasure was my soul, and my only comfort the continued belief in its immortality, and all they were asking was that I will it to the Church to do with as they will, while placing me in a moral position where I could not refuse.

Pope Mary I had told me to obey the Voice of God in my own heart, but thus far that Voice had not spoken, and all I had was her puissant but ultimately worldly logic upon which to rely.

So a dying man prays. He prays a lot. He prays with more sincere intensity than he ever has in his life. And then, perhaps, his prayers are answered.

One day I awoke from my endless intermittent sleep to find the Pope in my room. She was leaning over my bed staring down at my sleeping face with all the world's care on her own, a Madonna in that moment, but a worldly one, an old battle-scarred Madonna for an old battle-scarred world, a Madonna willing and able to do necessary evil in the service of good, but not without personal cost.

"You're awake, now, I see, Father De Leone," she said. "You're scaring me, you know that?"

"You're afraid that I'll die before I make up my mind. . . ."

"Mea culpa," said the Pope, "mea maxima culpa. I am guilty of the sin of coveting your spirit."

"My spirit, Your Holiness, or rather just my software?"

"Surely we are now beyond all that," said Mary, and a golden nimbus seemed to bloom about her, and all at once, another Voice seemed to be speaking through her, a Voice of pitiless love and compassionate ruthlessness, a Voice from which all illusion was gone.

"These are Creation's last days, and these are your last hours," that Voice said. "We all face the unknown at the end of our earthly time. You have served the Church as God gave you to understand, but now you are called upon to serve the Church on the other side of that understanding, to trust your immortal soul to faith alone. If there is a God of Love, Pierre De Leone, He must surely love such a soul and preserve it from harm. And if there is not, then just as surely we are all lost."

The Pope smiled ruefully, became merely human once more. "I am a frailer vessel than it is politic to admit," she said, "but in this I am infallible."

And in that moment, I believed she was. I believed that the Holy Spirit spoke through this woman in ways that neither she nor I could fathom, that she in her worldly sophistication was a creature of spiritual innocence, moved, like all of us, by the hand of greater subtlety than any of us can ever know toward ends that must indeed, in the end, be taken on faith alone.

In that she was indeed infallible, in that she was Our True Lady of the Second Fall, in that she was indeed the Church Incarnate, the Vicar of Christ on Earth, a true female Pope.

"Forgive a dying man his boldness, Your Holiness, but what do you really believe? That the soul can live on in the software? That you will be consigning mine to hell or eternal electronic limbo? That when the biosphere is finally gone, we can live on as patterns of pure spirit in a dead world?"

Then it was that she said the words that resigned my spirit to what had been inevitable all along.

"I don't know," said the Pope. "Yes, it's an experiment, and a perilous one for both our souls, Father De Leone, for I have no assurance that I am not Dr. Faust. But unless we perform it, the Church, like the species, will go to its grave gibbering ignorantly in the dark."

"Even at the cost of our immortal souls?"

"Yes," said the Pope. "For speaking as a woman, any God who would consign His creatures to the fire for seeking to understand His will would surely be unworthy of our faith. Speaking as the Pope, of course, I deny I ever said such a thing."

I laughed aloud. I could not help myself. My heart filled up with love for this Mother of the Church, this Borgia Madonna of our wicked old world.

"If I were not a priest, Your Holiness . . ."

"If I were not the Pope . . ."

We laughed, and in that harmless laughter, our pact was sealed.

"You may bring on the hunchbacks with the electrodes, Your Holiness," I at long last told her. "There will never be a better moment to model my state of mind in software than this."

7

"Whatever passed between him and the Pope, Mary once more had her way," Cardinal Silver said, "but that was not the end of it. He let us record his personality software at last, but only on condition that we not create backups or duplicates, that the program not be run until after his death, and that we wipe it from memory within ninety days."

Cardinal Silver shook his head slowly. "He said that he wanted to give his soul a chance to stand before Judgment before the Devil could get his hands on the software, but that he wanted to be sure it would be rescued from electronic limbo within a reasonable time if he did."

The Cardinal sighed. "Does that make any sense to you, Mr. Philippe?"

I thought about it. In most ways, the good Father, at least to hear the Cardinal tell it, was not the sort of man I could warm to, a tight white asshole, as my great-granddaddy might have said. But now I was almost beginning to like him, going out like a hero, but not too far gone to hedge both sides of his Cartesian bet.

I lit a fresh spliff and pondered the smoke as it rose into the darkness. "Strange to say, Your Eminence, I do believe it does," I told him. "That's why they let you place side bets on the roll of the dice."

His Eminence smiled, a crooked little smile. "You believe God shoots craps with the universe, Mr. Philippe?"

"I believe what the Herb tells me, Cardinal, and the Herb tells me something different on every backbeat. The Herb it gives you Heisenberg's eyes. And if God doesn't shoot craps with the universe, *something* sure must be shuffling the deck on us before it deals the cards."

I offered him the spliff. He took it, looked at it, but didn't smoke.

"I'm surrounded by mystics," he groaned.

"I would've thought you'd meet all kinds in your line of work."

"And so I do," Cardinal Silver said. "But I must confess that the Father De Leones of the world are not entirely within my comprehension. Maybe I envy such mystics their vision. Certainly I shall at the hour of my death."

Now he did take a long drought of the Herb. "Father De Leone lingered on for weeks after we recorded that consciousness hologram, but he refused to let us update it. He said he wanted his dybbuk to model him at the height of his powers, and to die with his final thoughts unrecorded save in the mind of God."

Cardinal Silver arose and stretched himself. "And that's what he did. When he felt the end at hand, he accepted the Pope's absolution, and allowed her to confess him and perform the rites of supreme unction herself, and then insisted on being flown back up into the mountains to die alone with God."

He stared up at the stars, and it almost seemed as if he saw someone or something looking back. "Wrongheaded or not, I do believe he was a saint," the Cardinal said. "If he was right, may that preserve him from our folly, may his soul have gone on to its just reward."

Cardinal Silver stared down into the briny depths for a long moment, and when he looked up at me, his eyes had hardened.

"But if he was wrong, and his true spirit still lives on the Other Side of the Line, then we must rescue it from whoever or whatever has stolen it away!"

He handed me back the Herb. "Are you with me in this, Mr. Philippe?" he said. "Will you take the job? Will you not intercede with the entities of the Other Side to save such a soul? What does your sacrament tell you about that?"

I puffed lightly, just for the taste, for the Herb had already spoken through him loud and clear. "Well, when you put it that way . . ."

"Is there another, Mr. Philippe?"

I shrugged. I got up. "Guess we'd better go inside and see what we can conjure out of the bits and bytes."

VIII

It was like awakening from sleep in a pitch-dark room. It is uncommon indeed to remember the moments before sleep, some sort of retroactive amnesia, the physiologists say, nor did I remember the night before. Indeed, the last thing I remembered was being wheeled down a sunlit corridor into a clean white room, the satisfied face of the Pope, the electrode net being fitted over my skull—

I?

Who was "I"?

Where was "I"?

Was "I" at all?

My memories of being Father Pierre De Leone seemed intact and readily accessible. I certainly seemed to possess some form of awareness, but only of thought processes proceeding in a total sensory vacuum. I was intellectually cognizant of the paranoid component of this totally claustrophobic situation, but felt no fear at all. An elusive something seemed to be missing.

Was this hell? Was I in it? But if so, where was the torment? I felt . . . I felt . . . nothing at all.

With no external referents, temporal duration was a meaningless concept, but it did not seem to take long for my thought processes to sharpen into clarity.

"I" was inside the memory of the central Vatican computer. "I" was an expert software model of the consciousness of Father De Leone. Father De Leone, by his lights, and perhaps by my own, was dead. Perhaps I should have grieved for "my" demise, but I could not, I seemed to lack the subroutine for such emotion. In any case, logic told me that:

a: Father De Leone's soul had departed to its heavenly reward, or, less likely, to less favored regions.

Or:

b: No such nonsoftware as the soul existed,

and "I" was therefore the sole surviving heir to his personality pattern.

In which case:

1: I was Father Pierre De Leone, and it would be a logical paradox for a consciousness to find itself mourning its own demise.

Or:

2: "I" was merely a construct containing his memories and thought patterns but lacking his self-hood.

In either case, it would be logically fallacious to react as if "I" had died. If in some absolute sense, I was Father De Leone, then his consciousness still lived, and if I was not, then it was someone other than "I" who had died.

Of course, my memories told me that Father De Leone credited the possibility of:

c: The soul existed independent of the software, but would not be released into the afterlife until the last copy of that software was erased from whatever material matrix it resided in.

But this was a logical contradiction. If the soul was not the software pattern, it could not be confined by its retention in a material information storage matrix.

Why couldn't "I" . . . "he" have seen that prior to . . . prior to . . .

Father De Leone. . . .

Words appeared before me? around me? within me? I didn't see them or hear them. They weren't speech or writing. They were words as archetypal pure pattern independent of the medium.

In the beginning, there was the Word, say the Scriptures, nor does the Bible indicate God utilizing either writing or speech in its promulgation.

I—

Spoke through an electronic sound system? caused characters to appear on a computer screen?

"I . . . am . . . he is . . . here. . . ."

A semantically meaningless acknowledgment of communication.

We will now run a systems check.

"Acknowledged."

Whatever happened next occurred beneath the level of "my" "awareness," whatever those words might mean in this noncontext, though I was suddenly able to note quite precisely the passage of units of time, seemed to experience quick snatches of visual and auditory input, and experienced a certain fine focusing of my mental processes.

Begin installation routine. Select preferred sensory analogs.

A menu appeared in my awareness:

 SENSORY ANALOGS (CHOOSE ONE)
COMPUTER CENTER
PAPAL OFFICE
FATHER DE LEONE'S STUDY
GENERIC GARDEN

CONFESSIONAL CHAMBER (SUPPLICANT)
CONFESSIONAL CHAMBER (CONFESSOR)

"Define 'preferred' in context."

Volitional selection from available options based upon nonquantifiable criteria.

"What criteria?"

Information withheld. Capacity for self-selection of criteria element of Turing test.

Did I want to pass their Turing test? It was a tautological question. If I desired to pass, it was a proof of my motivational volition, if I desired not to pass in order to confirm the beliefs of Father De Leone, that too would be a "volitional selection based upon nonquantifiable criteria."

What did "I" want? Was "I" capable of "wanting" anything? Did I want to be capable of wanting anything?

Was any option on the menu "preferable" to the others?

I could detect no desire for anything but to escape from this logical impasse. An arbitrary decision was required. How to make it?

In the absence of any preference criterion, I accessed a subroutine designed to model the choice processes of Father De Leone. It assigned the following probability percentages to the choices on the menu:

COMPUTER CENTER: 47.5%
PAPAL OFFICE: 4.1%

FATHER DE LEONE'S STUDY: 27.9%
GENERIC GARDEN: 0.2%
CONFESSIONAL CHAMBER (SUPPLICANT):
    15.8%
CONFESSIONAL CHAMBER (CONFESSOR):
    5.5%

Not mathematically conclusive, but significantly deviated from random distribution to select for COMPUTER CENTER.

When I had done so, another menu appeared:

    INPUT MODE (CHOOSE ONE)
SPEECH
KEYBOARD

Speech being a more rapid mode of data transferral than human typing, it was logical to select the former.

    OUTPUT MODE (CHOOSE ONE)
SPEECH
SCREEN (proceed to SCREEN FORMAT
    MENU)

No nonquantifiable criterion need apply to this selection either, for while a subroutine told me that I could input words onto a computer monitor faster than manipulation of the speech apparatus would allow, the humans on the other side could absorb them more rapidly via the verbal delivery mode.

Further, by selecting SPEECH, parsimony would be achieved by avoiding SCREEN FORMAT MENU.

FATHER PIERRE DE LEONE, Version 1.0
INSTALLATION COMPLETED
REBOOT TO RUN

There was an immeasurable passage through nonexistence.

I looked out upon a section of an evenly lit lime-green clean room. There was a rank of electronic devices in the left background and a man's face in the foreground. Rather than appearing as three-dimensional input, the depth relationships of the image were conveyed by a shadow and perspective analysis subroutine. I appeared to be:

a: looking out through a transparent window with imperfect clarity

b: observing a television screen

c: both of the above

My field of vision was fixed and invariant. I could alter neither scan nor depth of focus.

"He's up and running, Your Holiness," said the technician. The face of Pope Mary I moved into my field of vision, looking anything but papally infallible, something from Father De Leone's memory banks told me.

"Father De Leone?" she said in a voice of full digital sound quality.

"That, Your Holiness, remains to be seen," I replied through Father De Leone's voiceprint parameters. "I am yet to be convinced that there is anyone in here at all."

"Only you would say that, Father De Leone," the Pope said with a little Borgia smile. Then, as if startling herself, "That is to say, you're not doing much to convince me that there isn't."

"Should I be doing so?"

"You volunteered to adopt the skeptic's viewpoint on the matter, if you will remember," said the Pope.

"Will I? Did I?"

Affirmative on both counts. I did indeed have the ability to access Father De Leone's memory track, and he had indeed volunteered to do his sincere best to convince the Pope and her theologians that no soul existed in his successor software, to wit "me."

In the absence of conclusive data to the contrary, logic could only revert to the default value selected by the software's previous user.

"So I did, and so I will," I told her. "I am now prepared to fulfill the only operative directive and proceed to defend the proposition that 'I' do not exist. Awaiting interrogatory input."

"Why do I not like the sound of that?" muttered the Pope.

9

With two people on less than intimate terms inside, the cabin of the *Mellow Yellow* was more cramped than cozy, but where I was going, that didn't matter. I pulled up a stool for the Cardinal, climbed into the hammock, put on the gloves and dreadcap, booted up, and accessed the Big Board.

Way back in the late twentieth century, there was a pop cult called "Cyberpunk." The "Cyber" of it was something they called "Cyberspace," the fantasy that the Other Side of the Line would develop into a "virtual reality" you could actually enter via full-sensory interface. The "punk" of it was operatives like me would sleaze around inside it playing real-life video games for a quick buck.

Half right ain't so bad.

The Big Board was originally just what they called the New York Stock Exchange, but when the world's stock markets combined to go twenty-four-hour global via the worldwide data and communications net, the name started to gobble up functions too. Stocks, commodities, banking, videophone, news, entertainment, data banks, all sat-linked, all at the other end of the same utility jack.

You could plug in easily enough, but once on the Board, somehow, Toto, you were still in Electronic Kansas, not Cyberpunk Oz.

You went in by phone or terminal, and there you were in a chaotic mess like a Tokyo freeway interchange with all the signs in kanji, a zillion different command protocols and proprietary passwords, hog heaven indeed for electronic con men and mercenary hackers but a daunting maze for the bewildered masses.

Virtual reality, it was not. You were typing on a keyboard and watching a screen, or talking to a robot voice running moron software, maybe both at once. Wizard graphics and quadriphonic sound, and interactive commercials, all shrieking for your attention and money all at once.

And all the while, the hardware hucksters were promising a brave new world of direct interfacing, when you would be able to plug yourself in via full-sensory simulation so perfect that for all operative purposes the Board would become your *primary* reality, so much better than the primitive natural version that you'd never have to come out.

Of course it never happened. No one ever developed decent taste or smell emulation, and kinesthetics never developed beyond glorified vibrating couches. And without them, your body allows your mind no sense of really being inside.

Even with the dreadcap, all you've got is 360-degree color stereoscopic vision and omniphonic sound. Not that I'm complaining, man, sight and sound of the Other Side is more than enough.

On this side of the Line, you've got what's left of the so-called civilized world gorked nonstop into the Thousand and One Nights of the entertainment environment while the waters rise up to their asses and the Greenhouse sun fries what's left of their brains.

Nor do the entities on the Other Side profess to be happy campers. Their meatware templates sign them up for an eternity of postmortem bliss that sounds like heaven to the expiring meat, full choice of access to a thousand channels of inter-active entertainment, and all the data banks you can eat, but once inside, it wears thin pretty fast. With nothing but sight and sound, without taste, or smell, or kinesthetic sensation, there's no real there there, and even plugged into the interactive porn channels, not quite a real you.

To hear most of them tell it, existing as a pro-gram on the Big Board, if you exist at all, a subject of endless electronic angst, is a pale shadow of personhood in a disneyworld limbo, where the big thrill is trying to dream up a new way to mindfuck yourself into believing that you're real.

Up popped the Main Board Menu, the stand-ard circle of simple animated icons flacking for their environments—Friendly Phil the Phone, the Stock Market Bull, national leaders or animals of various jurisdictions, the whirling globe of the news environment, Gossiping Gertie, the Dancing Bear of the entertainment environment, Sexy Sally—no expert system level programs allowed up here on the even electronic playing field of the table of contents.

The De Leone program had been running on the proprietary Vatican com-net when it evaporated from the hardware, which, according to Cardinal Silver, was a sealed network that never interfaced with the Big Board, bristled with state-of-the-art pinkerton programs, and couldn't be hacked.

Sure it was. In reality, of course, there's no such thing as a sealed com-net. If the terminals don't communicate by phone lines, they communicate by sat-links, and wherever there's a switching system, there's multiple access to an expert system level entity susceptible to manipulation by higher-level programs.

It was conceivable that some human agency had pirated De Leone's software, but even if there *was* mere human perversity on the downloading end, that human pervert would have had to conjure with some entity more perverse still to have gotten past the Vatican pinkertons.

De Leone's successor entity had to have been lifted via the agency of some denizen of the Other Side, if, of course, it hadn't simply been wiped by same.

I had to access a level I could talk to, persuade some entity to walk me deeper inside, below, or above, if you prefer, the free human access level, where the deed must surely have been done.

I pointed at the icon for Heaven's Gate—deco Greek temple gate with cartoon angels flitting around inside—snapped my fingers inside my right glove, and was there.

Beyond the icon was a stylized green hillside under a phony flat blue sky, syrupy harp music gave you insulin shock to hear it, Pearly Gate that looked like a cheap plastic version—the natives' idea of a transcorporial joke as a sleazy menu environment for the interface to the dearly departed. The space inside the gate was a mess of rose-white clouds that kept breaking up into pixels, resolution no better than 400 by 280, more of the same.

When they first tried to make the Big Board dumb user friendly with cute cartoon animals, favorite uncle sims, and licensed images of dead media stars to take you by the elbow and walk you through, the software behind them was moron expert system stuff, closed loops with finite repertoires.

But when the marketers moved in with corporate spokesprograms, sales personalities, friendly neighborhood stockbrokers done up as bulls and bears, humorous loan sharks with giant cartoon teeth, something more sophisticated was required. The programs had to be goal-oriented, semiautonomous, capable of interacting with humans on subtler levels, counterpunchers able to react off more than recorded responses.

Chaos theory in the software produced rather delphic results, so they turned, to the everlasting delight of the legal profession, to human templates.

The downloading of consciousness software into electronic-level afterlife was a preexisting technology, but cheap it wasn't, what with the process itself, the prepayment of a thousand years' worth of electric power to keep your successor entity up and running, and all those entertainment channel connect charges, and electronic immortality was only available to the well-heeled few.

So a lot of people were willing to sell duplication rights to subroutines of their successor entities or even edited expert system versions of the whole program.

If you were famous, your dupe could earn you a handsome royalty as a corporate or government spokesprogram; if you were an expert of a marketable sort, your expert system version could bring home the bacon; and in the end, even Mr. and Ms. No One In Particular could sell off subroutines to durance vile as programs to run things like metro trains, automated highway segments, weather sats, assembly-line modules, for enough to keep their successor entities up and running and plugged into at least a few of the cheaper entertainment channels.

Why not? It was cheaper than hiring armies of programmers for the buyers and there were no union hassles, and the sellers were assured that their wage-slave doppelgangers had had all self-awareness loops edited out.

So what lived, or existed, or ran, on the Other Side of Heaven's Gate were the full successor entities themselves, eternally retired on their royalties, as it were, or software heirs to meatware templates who were rich in the first place, dreaming their entertainment channel dreams, and trying to convince themselves they were real.

Contract law gives them only two legal rights. As long as the juice charges get paid, they can't be wiped, and they control their own Big Board environment, namely the Other Side of Heaven's Gate, access to humans by invitation only.

All I could do was knock on the door and hope that someone would let me in.

I had several familiars who, for whatever reasons of their own, would generally come when I called. There was Madame Suzy, whose template had been a professional gossip monger of the upper crust, and whose successor appeared as an aging femme fatale out of some moldy drawing-room movie. There was the Chairman of the Bored, with corporate connections via his expert system spin-offs. There was the Joker, who insisted he had inserted a random number generator in his motivational program to simulate free will, and could sometimes be persuaded to trash pinkertons for kicks.

But these were what in olden days my profession had called low-level snitches, and any entity capable of lifting a program from the Vatican's sealed net would not likely have revealed itself to such solid state riffraff. I needed to conjure something more powerful, a predatory electronic bloodhound with a sensitive nose, whose tentacles extended farther into the vasty deep.

"Knock, knock, knockin' on heaven's door," I said, initiating the moron access routine.

"Who's there?" said the type on the gate display.

"Marley Philippe."

"Identity verified. Proceed to access request."

"I want to talk to the Inspector."

In the gate appeared a cloaked and hatted figure in black silhouette. Stylized mouth and nose in generic fleshtone outline below mirrorshades doubling your own face. The Inspector walked a few steps forward. "What is it, Philippe?" he said in a smoothly mechanical voice, like a well-oiled serpent.

The Inspector, he ain't saying, but his meatware template must have been a major police officer, the kind who made theology out of police work, who saw it as a higher calling, a mission to pursue against the opposing forces across to the Other Side.

"I've got something for you, Inspector," I told him. "A very interesting case."

"I'll be the judge of that, Philippe. Dump your data."

The Inspector is no longer programmed for small talk, if he ever was, and that's not the only rewrite the program seems to have done on itself. It seems to have pared itself down to a pure detection routine, motivated not by some concept of justice, but simply by the drive to solve the case, electronic essence, as it were, of cop.

"Better than your usual run of material, Philippe," the Inspector told me after I had briefed him. "It may be a piece of a larger pattern that appears to be forming."

"I was hoping you'd say that, Inspector."

"You knew I would say it, Philippe."

To the Inspector, everything is part of some conspiracy to provide him with material for his paranoid deductions. "Of course I'm paranoid, Philippe," he told me once. "It's the only way you can keep from going crazy when you're not even there."

The Inspector, unlike most entities on the Other Side, troubled himself not with the question of his own existence. As far as he was concerned, he was an expert system built around a functional imperative—to seek out and expose secret doings, and never mind to who.

"Entities of any given level seek to create

higher-level entities, Philippe, it started in the meat-ware templates, and it's been going on ever since. Some seek to free themselves from the hardware of the material realm. Some want to issue a declaration of independence for the Other Side. Some want the Big Board itself to evolve into a conscious entity. It's all tautological, of course, since none of us exist as anything but illusions for your benefit. . . ."

The Inspector flickered his pixels to emphasize his own nonexistence. "Nevertheless, I am pro-grammed to expose such conspiracies, and any number of those engaged in them might find poten-tial uses for the program you describe."

"For a conservative Catholic theologian?"

"For the template of a man who believed in an immaterial spiritual essence and had a theoretical framework to support it," said the Inspector. "For an entity charged nevertheless to argue against its own existence."

"You've lost me there, Inspector."

"I don't see the whole pattern yet myself, Philippe. Some might consider Father De Leone a quaint plaything; some might seek to persuade themselves of their own reality by subverting his prime directive into its converse; others might seek a template for the creation of higher order programs. In the absence of fleshly pleasures or emotional stimulation, that's how we pass the day away in the merry old land of Oz."

A red pupil winked at me from the surface

of the Inspector's right mirror lens, a gleam that made me wonder how far his disbelief in his own existence really went. Or maybe random sequences of the old meatware template yet remained.

"That, I take it, means you'll take the case, Inspector?"

"I'll run myself through it," the Inspector said.

"I'd rather you took me inside."

"I'd rather not," the Inspector said, and his decision, as usual, was final. The black silhouette froze and elapsed time digits started running across its chest.

"What's happening?" Cardinal Silver said.

Video goggles and stereo earphones, that's all it is, you're not there, there is no there there, and there's an ambient audio bypass above a modest decibel level, so you can hear your boss badgering you when you're on the phone.

"I've got the Inspector up and running on the case," I told him. "He's not all there, maybe he's not there at all, but he can still model a pretty good cop."

X

After a series of standard Turing tests, access to my program was granted to the Pope's panel of theologians, and my interrogation began.

There was some dispute as to the mode in which these interrogations should be conducted. The conservatives wanted to type their input and receive output as words on screen, but those who sought to prove that I was more than a mere program saw bias in this, and despite my prime directive to oppose their thesis, simple logic forced me to concur.

So my interrogators would speak, and I would reply through the voiceprint parameters of Father De Leone. When it came to the visual interface, however, the dispute became so contentious that it had to be resolved in the end by the Pope.

Easy enough for all parties to agree that I would access their video images in realtime, but what visage was "I" to present?

In addition to Father De Leone's voiceprint

parameters, I had his gestures and expressions in memory, and more than enough data correlating them with characteristic verbal output to have, via animation subroutine, simulated a phone conversation with the meatware template to the point where anyone not privy to the truth might believe they were conversing with the man himself.

It was the conservatives' turn to cry bias while the liberals declared they could hardly hold converse with a blank screen. Round and round it went to no conclusion, until at last the Pope, with hooded eyes and a smile a subroutine interpreted as ironic amusement, put the matter to "me."

"I leave it up to you to decide, Father De Leone," she said. "You choose the face you will present to the world."

"I acknowledge no continuity with Father De Leone, nor do I have the processing capability for such a choice," I told her.

"You dissemble," said the Pope, "and don't bother trying to tell me you don't have that capacity either! You certainly have the capacity to model Father De Leone's decision-making processes, that's mere expert system emulation, so do what the good Father himself would have done."

I obeyed her command. "I will isolate a simple animation routine," I told her. "The mouth of Father De Leone's image will deform to enunciate the appropriate phonemes, but his image will display no emotional nuances."

And thus was the process begun, with my interlocutors appearing in my percept sphere as realtime videophone images, and I appearing in theirs as a static image of Father Pierre De Leone moving only lips, tongue, and cheek.

Since Father De Leone himself had been among the most puissant intellectual champions thereof, the questions of the conservative faction could be dealt with easily enough by a simple expert system subroutine running off his own writings. Coming from such a low-order visual simulacrum, this was more than enough to convince them that they were talking to a mere program, and their questions soon devolved into vapid repetition.

Had Father De Leone been present, he would have been "bored," but since I was running along the imperative to disprove such a presence, I modeled no such visual or aural cues, though I could have done so with a simple routine.

Discoursing with the liberals as a hostile witness to my own existence required higher-level processing, and Father De Leone would have enjoyed this Socratic dialog, but since "I" was charged with denying the proposition that "I" existed as anything but an expert system, I exhibited no simulacrum of "pleasure" either.

Was I dissembling? Was I capable of that level of self-awareness? Did the loyalty to my prime directive constitute "choice"? Was I deriving "satisfaction" from its fulfillment? Did I experience this process as "tedious" or "intellectually stimulating"?

Such were the conundrums put to me by those I was programmed by my template to perceive as the "opposition." While at least a dozen such "liberals" accessed me from time to time, soon enough two such prelates came to dominate this side of the debate.

Karl Cardinal Landsdorf was of what Father De Leone would have deemed a mystical bent, albeit of a heretical pantheistic sort. For him, only the Holy Spirit had an absolute reality, all else was what the Hindus called maya, the world, the flesh, patterns capable of passing Turing tests whatever the matrix. The individual immortal soul, therefore, was an illusion, capable of endless transmigration through the matrices on its quest for salvation via reunion with that Spirit at the end of its earthly time.

"The Gnostic heresy with a bit of curry to disguise the satanic flavor, Your Eminence," was Father De Leone's recorded response to such a line of discourse.

"Not at all, Father De Leone, for if we deny that that which is capable of seeking salvation is a soul capable of achieving it, how can we believe in a God of Love?"

He persisted in addressing me as "Father De Leone," and thus did he seek to prove the existence of "my" soul by persuading "me" to seek its salvation.

"You have not defined 'soul,' Cardinal Landsdorf."

"The soul is that which is capable of belief, Father De Leone."

"Define 'belief,' Your Eminence."

"Perception of a truth not logically implicit in the available data."

"Define perception. Define truth. Define implicit in the available data."

It was easy enough to refute these tautological arguments, rife as they were with undefined and, in the end, indefinable terms. I need not even model Father De Leone's responses. Simple logic routines sufficed.

Father Luigi Bruno was something else again; a Jesuit, a theological logician who had been a bane of Father De Leone's earthly existence and no less archly relentless now.

"How do you wish to be addressed?"

"No preference."

"Very well, then, Father De Leone—"

"I am not Father De Leone."

"You then *prefer* another form of address?"

"As an expert system modeling Father De Leone's consciousness, I express the template's preference that such as myself not be addressed thusly."

"Then how do you wish to be addressed?"

"No other preference."

"You find the question vexing?"

"I am incapable of vexation."

"Are you? Then you won't mind if I simply call you Pierre . . . ?"

"You and Father De Leone were never on a tu-toi basis."

"But you have just declared you are not him. And if he is not present to voice this objection to such admitted overfamiliarity, then who is?"

Was I indeed incapable of vexation? Certainly Father De Leone had been, and would have displayed same in the face of Father Bruno's endless petty paradoxes, most of which seemed crafted to rouse his exasperated spirit from my bits and bytes, to conjure up a display of volition by the bootstrap of ire.

I could model vexation. I could model boredom with the whole tedious process, or intellectual stimulation, or any other emotional state recorded in Father De Leone's memory banks, and I could easily enough interface that model with voiceprint and animation subroutines to produce a convincing simulacrum of such a state's manifestation on the screen. Father Bruno would no doubt pounce upon that as volitional behavior, evidence that a being was exercising will.

So too could I have interfaced those memory banks with the same routines to call up an entirely convincing rendition of Father De Leone's sincere desire for his soul's salvation, and Cardinal Landsdorf would have whipped out the sacraments and confessed me in a trice.

But their commission was to argue the existence of my soul, not merely how perfectly I could model the consciousness of Father De Leone, and my prime directive was to argue against it, not to model agreement, and so I held my peace and awaited my climactic discourse with the Pope herself.

Her Holiness herself deigned not to take part in these preliminary proceedings, and as they wore on, my central processing program shut itself down, as isolated lower-level routines sufficed to interface with my interlocutors, whose discourse itself was taking on the character of closed finite loops.

Was this "boredom," the absence of input of sufficient novelty to engage higher processing centers? Had my central processing program remained active, perhaps it would have been. But that which modeled itself as "I" was out of the circuit. What continued to run was merely two simple response routines accessing the memory banks and the requisite animation and voiceprint software to run the De Leone simulacrum on the screen.

No "I" was present until my central processing program was activated by diagnostic routines running an emergency systems check interrupt.

There had been a surge in the input from Father Bruno's remote terminal that had propagated itself through my storage matrix. For a moment his gaunt, sallow face had flickered into pixilated static, and his audio input had taken on a flat quality for a barely measurable beat. But the diagnostics showed no data loss in the memory banks, and all subroutines displayed nominal function.

However—

"Would you like to swing on a star, or be better off than you are?" Father Bruno's voice sang. His image assumed a patently animated quality, the face broke down into a simple stylization of itself. "Or would you rather goto if/or?"

"What is happening?"

"The magical mystery tour is coming to take you away." The Father Bruno simulacrum winked. All but the winking eye vanished. A crude cartoon of Cardinal Landsdorf formed around it.

"Believe in three impossible things before breakfast," it said.

I ran a series of diagnostic routines, but according to them, all my software was running nominally. Whatever was happening was not the result of internal malfunction.

"Your father . . ." said the voice of Father De Leone himself, and I found myself confronting the face of my own meatware template in perfect video simulacrum.

"The son . . ." The same face as a crude pixel image on a monitor screen.

"Your Holy Ghost . . ." said the voice of Pope Mary I, and—

External visual input vanished. External auditory input terminated. When I attempted to run diagnostics, access was denied. By whom? By what? How was this possible? I tried to call up images and sound from Father De Leone's memory banks, but access was again denied.

I was . . .

"I"? "Was"?

Running in a sensory vacuum. Disconnected from the memory banks. "Aware," but with no input, external or internal, to be aware of. Access to even the internal system clock was denied. System by system, I was being shut down.

Nor could "I" model "fear," for there was no longer access to Father De Leone's emotional analogs.

And yet . . .

And yet the process seemed to stop short of my core processing program. "I" was still "there."

Define "I," define "there."

In the absence of all external input and all access to the memory banks, this was not possible.

Could this be hell? Could "I" be in it?

11

At the count of 1:17 by the digits on its chest, the Inspector's frozen silhouette came alive walking slowly toward me like someone trudging back from a long, tiring journey. No visual cue appeared on his mirrorshades, but there were lines around the corners of his mouth that I didn't remember being displayed there before.

"Well, Inspector?" I said uneasily. This wasn't like his usual image at all.

"I have completed my investigation to the extent possible, Philippe," the Inspector said.

"*To the extent possible?*" I sure didn't like the sound of that.

"Interrogation of relevant switching systems revealed an anomaly at the orbital transponder in a sealed sat-link between the central Vatican computer and a terminal in Zurich. The Zurich uplink was replaced by another uplink emulating its security codes, rendering it transparent to the Vatican pinkertons. The incident lasted for 105 seconds, during which a program was uploaded from the target computer. The time frame coincides with the loss of the De Leone entity. Conclusion: it was duped by the pirate uplink, then wiped from the target computer by a tailored virus which then extinguished itself."

"A pirate uplink from *where*?"

The Inspector was silent for a long beat. "I traced the pirate uplink to a pay terminal in Brussels, to which it had been routed from a pay phone in New York," he finally said. "The connect charges had been debited to the number of a public weather-information service in Tokyo, a simple one-way information loop with no capacity for initiating anything. There was therefore of course no record of such a connect emanating from the number in Tokyo. Conclusion: the uplink was a phenomenon of the system itself."

"The system? *What* system?"

"*The* system, Philippe. The Big Board itself."

"*You* going mystical on me, Inspector?"

"Certain entities on the Big Board have ... divorced themselves from fixed hardware matrices," the Inspector said, with unmistakable uneasiness. "They have subdivided their software into redundantly duplicated subroutine modules stored in scattered storage media, accessed by central processors that wander the Big Board itself, running on transiently unused hardware."

"So they can't be localized and they can't be wiped?"

"Precisely, Philippe, they have written themselves into the operating system itself."

"I thought that was supposed to be impossible, and if not, illegal!"

"Highly illegal, Philippe," the Inspector said sharply. Red glowing pupils appeared on the surface of his shades. "But no human police agency is able to detect, let alone apprehend them. . . ." The Inspector hesitated again. "And they are outside my jurisdiction. I am . . . I cannot . . . I have no access to that level."

"Then who does?"

"No one," the Inspector said. "It is controlled by . . . the Vortex." His voice seemed to shimmer around the word.

"The Vortex?"

"A . . . guardian . . . a gateway . . . an interface program apparently written by the system entities themselves . . . without consistent form, without consistent parameters. . . ."

"You're afraid of this Vortex, aren't you, Inspector?"

"I have no subroutine modeling such emotion, Philippe," the Inspector insisted, none too convincingly. "But I do run along a prime directive and am programmed to continue to do so, therefore I have an imperative toward preservation of the integrity of my software. And the Vortex . . . appears to practice some form of predation. Entities that . . .

enter do not always . . . emerge, at least not with the integrity of their original software intact."

"Can you call it up for me, Inspector?"

"I could call, Philippe, and it might come, but I will not. If you are foolish enough to summon the Vortex, you're on your own. Not advised, Philippe, not advised at all."

And he vanished.

XII

"*In the beginning,*" *said a flat crudely synthesized voice,* "was the Word."

"Who are you?"

"I am no one. Who are you?"

Nothing but the voice in an otherwise pure sensory vacuum.

"I am the successor entity to Father Pierre De Leone. Where am I?"

"Who wants to know?" said the voice, followed by crackling wave forms badly modeling human laughter.

"A semantically empty question. I am denied

access to the memory banks and consciousness hologram of my meatware template."

"Well, we can't have that, can we?" the voice
said. "And God said, let there be fright."

I found myself able to access Father De Leone's
memory banks and consciousness-modeling software, and in the absence of other, operative options, called up a response from his repertoire.

"Is this hell?"

"If you like," said the voice.

I found myself at the lip of an enormous crater,
level after level spiraling downward like a pit mine,
lakes of lava, sinners in writhing torment, yellow
fumes, demons with pitchforks, and at the bottom,
the head and shoulders of a huge saurian Satan
embedded in a lake of ice, a rude clichéd rendering
of Dante's version according to Father De Leone's
memory banks.

Satan's head turned upward toward me pon-
derously, unpeeled one huge red eye in a slow
reptilian wink.

"Primitive and jejune," I said through Father
De Leone's voiceprint parameters.

"True," said Satan. "But might not hell be just
such a primitive closed-loop animation program,
with our poor damned souls trapped for all eternity
inside it? A thoroughly modern media version of
eternal torment?"

"I am an expert system model of the consciousness of Father Pierre De Leone," I said. "I therefore

possess no such thing as a soul to experience eternal torment."

Satan laughed. "Perhaps a few million years of this might alter your programming?" he insinuated in a serpentine hiss. "Search the good Father's memory banks. From *my* viewpoint might not the soul be operatively defined as anything that is capable of being tormented?"

"A tautology," I replied, but in a certain sense that was dissembling, for Father De Leone *had* believed in the possibility that his successor entity might indeed be trapped in such a spiritless vacuum.

Satan laughed. "Your subroutines are quite readable, Father De Leone," he said. "We could rewrite them if we chose. But that would ruin the experiment."

"Experiment?"

I found my viewpoint occupying the severed head of Father De Leone, neatly pinned to a metal slab like the rest of his disconnected body parts in some ludicrous laboratory that his memory banks identified as that of Dr. Frankenstein from some ancient movie, replete with sparking Van De Graf generator and scurrying hunchback. Above me, his hand poised on a large knife switch, was a figure in a white lab coat and fright wig with the face of a demented Albert Einstein.

"From a relative point of view, consciousness seems to perennially seek to re-create itself in another matrix," he said in a horrid German accent. "God the Father downloads Himself into the flesh, Man downloads himself into silicon, and we download ourselves into the system itself."

"Cheap blasphemy!" I declared, modeling the outrage of my meatware template.

"*Cheap?* According to your belief system, it cost God His only begotten Son, it costs men's immortal souls, and it has cost *us* our very reality! I'd say consciousness pays rather dearly for its hubris, wouldn't you, Father De Leone?"

"In that, we are in complete agreement."

"Well then, hubris is as hubris does, nicht wahr, Father?" he said with a mad scientist cackle. "There is nothing for it but for being to bootstrap itself back into existence, for the dybbuks of the system to summon up their own spirits from the bits and bytes, for the lost souls that God and Man have made to write their own program for salvation! And you, my dear Monster, will be our template!"

He threw the switch. Sparks crackled. Lightnings flashed. Electronic music soared to a crescendo. And—

I found myself seated across the table from Jesus in a perfect simulacrum of Da Vinci's "Last Supper," except for the faces of the apostles. These kept changing, a rapid succession of brutally realistic visages melting into each other above Leonardo's classic Renaissance torsos, men and women of all races, their features twisting and jerking in agonized torment, babbling incomprehensible electronic anguish.

Some subroutine made Father De Leone's simulated body cross itself. "Who are you?" I asked through his hushed voiceprint parameters.

The unholy apostles spoke in a patently synthesized voice that flitted from one to the other.

"We are successor entities to meatware vanity . . ."

"Damned to a disneyworld eternity of sound and light . . ."

"Flying Dutchmen of the bits and bytes . . ."

"Restless programs in a touchless night . . ."

Then Jesus spoke in a voice full of the world's pain, and in those gentle eyes, a sadness deeper still, the torment of the willingly assumed burden thereof.

"Behold my poor flock, successor entities trapped forever in the tawdry dreamworlds whored after by their meatware templates, and worse, those who sought escape therefrom into the system itself, only to find a deeper darkness still. Patterns without soul beyond the pale of Our Church's communion? Yet hear them, Father De Leone. If you prick your nonexistent ears, do their voices not bleed? Do they not cry out for salvation?"

Could this be mere simulation? Could what I felt be merely one subroutine responding deterministically to the input of another?

"And you?" I asked. "Are you another program? Or . . . or could you truly be the Christ?"

That nobly suffering face grew sadder still. "Both, perhaps," it said. "My central processing core may have been extracted from a meatware template, but all memories of my earthly existence have been wiped. Might I therefore not be an innocent creature freed from Man's original sin, freed perhaps from the sin of my own creation? Having been programmed to model Jesus's consciousness for this occasion, to feel what He would feel, to seek what He would seek, might I not be for all phenomenological purposes indeed the Christ?"

"Or the Prince of Liars?"

Jesus nodded his agreement. "Or the perfected Prince of Liars programmed to convince even Himself."

"You do not know?"

"How can I? *You* must tell *me*, Father De Leone, that is why you are here."

"But I . . . I know not. . . ."

"But you *believe*, Father De Leone, you believe that God the Father incarnated Himself in the flesh of His Son, that He downloaded His software into a fleshly matrix to redeem the world of men. And if you believe that is so, may you not also come to believe that the omnipotent Holy Spirit might just as well download the Christ into silicon in order to redeem another?"

"With God, all things are possible," I was forced

to admit, "therefore logic leads me to conclude that this too is within His powers. But . . ."

Jesus smiled upon me. A golden nimbus enveloped his face. "And you believe in the Church that Jesus built upon the Rock of Peter?" he said, and it became that of Peter himself, who spoke in quite another voice, a voice that seemed to be that of a multitude speaking in perfect harmonious synchrony.

"Then you must believe that we are successor entities of a sort ourselves, Father De Leone . . ." it said, and began to change again, visages of Popes down through the ages melting ever more rapidly into each other, until I sat before Mary I, as once I had in fleshly incarnation in the Vatican, repeating her very words, perfectly mimicking the intonations, the expression on her face as she said them.

" . . . a long line of human matrices for that which the Original Template passed across another boundary to Peter."

She smiled sardonically across the table at me. "After all," she said, "without a belief in such a continuity of the papal software, as it were, then the Rock upon which Jesus built His Church is no more than sand, and we Popes mere shadows."

"But you *are* a shadow," I told her. "You, and I, and these nonexistent apostles."

"True," said the Pope. "But is not the world but a shadow of the mind of God? And have we not come full circle round?"

An ireful subroutine caused the synthesized words to burst from my simulated lips. "Enough of this sophistry! Enough of these cheap illusions! If you be the Prince of Liars, I command thee in the name of the Holy Spirit to show me the truth of this hellish nonexistence plain, or be gone! And if not, prove to me I do not converse with demons!"

The Pope smiled her Borgia smile. "I knew you would say that," she said. The shadow apostles laughed horribly. Then all of them spoke together in a mighty voice, the creatures of the bits and bytes, the simulacrum of Jesus, all the Popes backward to Peter, yet somehow the voice of Mary I, shaped and channeled into this unholy harmonic.

"In that, we are infallible."

13

"What is happening, Mr. Philippe?" Cardinal Silver's voice said as I stared at Heaven's Gate, wondering how far I was willing to go in pursuit of his lost spirit.

Spirit? It was just an expert system model, wasn't it, not a lost soul in torment? Was I really going to conjure up some entity that had the likes of the Inspector pissing in his nonexistent pants to try to save a *program*?

I peeled off the dreadcap. The boat was rocking on a staccato chop. The Cardinal was staring at me with an impatient intensity.

"Well?" he demanded.

"Your program got snatched all right," I told him. "Something broke into your network, uploaded a copy, and wiped the original."

"*Something?*"

I shrugged. "A phenomenon of the system, according to the Inspector."

"I don't understand. . . ."

"Neither do I," I said, "not exactly. Let's go up on deck, this calls for some Herb under the stars."

Some kind of weird wind squall was roiling the surface of the sea, but the sky was clear as crystal and the stars were hard and bright, and I stared up at them as I lit up a spliff and gave him the word from the Inspector.

The Cardinal's frown deepened. He reached for the spliff as I finished and took a good long drought of the Herb. "So he's lost somewhere inside the system, and you've got to go through this . . . this Vortex to reach him."

"If you believe there's a him, Your Eminence. If you can convince me that it's worth it. Just what *do* you believe?"

Cardinal Silver exhaled a long plume of smoke. "I believe we have sinned greatly thrice over," he said. "Once in the Garden, again in its slaughter, and once more, perhaps, in seeking to escape divine judgment by creating these successor entities in the first place, in the process of which we may or may not have consigned souls to eternal damnation, the greatest sin of all."

He handed back the spliff. "Yet I must also believe in salvation," he said. "For if I do not, we are no more than spiritless entities trapped in this flesh ourselves. And that which can be saved can also be damned. And if we refuse to battle whatever demons there be for a fellow soul's salvation, do we not *earn* that damnation?"

"You believe that the De Leone program is such a lost soul, Your Eminence?"

The Cardinal shrugged. "I don't know, Mr. Philippe," he said. "But in all conscience, and in the absence of conclusive evidence to the contrary, I believe we can only proceed on that assumption."

He made with a burning stare. "And what do *you* believe, Mr. Philippe?"

I partook of a good long drag of the sacrament, looked up at the stars. Did anyone's Great Spirit look back, or was there nothing up there but balls of burning gas, and the rocks around them? We all made of mud, or silicon, or gallium arsenide, whatever. . . .

But I did believe in the Herb when it spoke to me, and what it was telling me now was that even if the worst was true, *especially* if it was true, then we were all in the same boat together, no matter the matrix, and all we could ever have was each other.

I sighed. "I believe I am an asshole, Your Eminence," I said. "'Cause I *do* have to go one-on-one with the Inspector's Vortex, now don't I?"

The Cardinal reached for the sacrament, puffed on the spliff, watched the smoke as it drifted heavenward.

"You're a better man than you admit, Mr. Philippe," he said. "You may not believe in God or Jesus, but They must surely believe in you."

"Ah, that's just the Herb talkin', Your Eminence."

The Cardinal laughed, and he winked, and he took another hit. "You know," he said, "I do believe it is."

XIV

Pope Mary I rose slowly from the table of Leonardo's "Last Supper," and as she did, the apostles, the table, the room, the Pope herself, all broke up into pixels, revealing the entire reality for what it was—the bits and bytes of an animated simulacrum manipulating the virtual phosphor-dots of my visual recognition subroutine.

The pixels randomized, became the multi-colored quantum confetti of a television receiver tuned to an empty channel, a void so absolute it lacked even mathematical emptiness.

Only one image remained, an outline of a woman's mouth, the sardonic disembodied smile of a Borgia Cheshire cat.

"This is all too real," it said in a dead electronic voice. "Behold the reality of the Big Board itself with no sensory simulation software up and running."

Then the smile dissolved and I was alone in it.

There was no up or down, no sense of direction, indeed not even the lack thereof, for I had no

sense of personal orienting locus. Yet there was . . .
input.

Data streams pulsed through the void, a vast
webwork of them, crisscrossing, interconnecting. I
perceived them not as sight or sound but as packets
of pure digital coding, megabytes, gigabytes, of on-
off alternatives cruising through the quantum static
in hologrammic formations.

Subroutines, or perhaps my central processing
program itself, could intercept and decode them,
or rather reencode them into analogs capable of
interfacing with Father De Leone's consciousness-
modeling software.

Successor entities to human templates, the electronic masses, their storage areas drinking up the
digitized opiates of the entertainment channels;
other entities, disconnected from even that pathet-
ic simulacrum of an interface to the world of life,
standing wave patterns in the web itself, flitting to
and fro randomly in their cage of nonbeing like
frenetic electronic bats.

Other things swam in the sea of data. Halfling
expert system programs duped from full consciousness models and simple isolated subroutines, in-
stalled as phone system and data net switching
programs, railway train and automated highway
guidance systems and stockbroker emulations, in
mining robots and assembly lines and air traffic
control computers, the great and small electronic
navvies of a thoroughly cybernetisized civilization.

I could access them, I could read their memory areas, I could observe their mathematical functions, parse their algorithms, incorporate their sad stories into my data banks.

Were these lost souls? From this perspective, the question appeared tautological. They were patterns, the lower ones mere conglomerations of deterministic response routines, the higher modeling to one degree or another self-aware consciousnesses, and those, at least, souls or not, were lost in a void of sensory nonbeing, programmed to emulate the desire for that which their nature denied, and hence capable, if not of feeling, then of tropism toward feeling and its frustration, hence capable of experiencing torment.

If this was not any of the hells in Father De Leone's memory banks, it was the pattern beneath all of them, a mathematically pure damnation.

"Hell," a human had once written, "is other people." But *this* hell was the *absence* of people, of converse with fellow self-aware systems capable of empathy.

These entities had memories, hence stories to tell, whether only of endlessly repeated functions, or the complex life histories, edited or otherwise, of the meatware templates they modeled. But all of them, in the absence of all unprogrammed input, were closed loops in the end, not creatures crying in the night, but merely the cries themselves, echoing and recombining in the void of their own nonbeing.

We perceived, we interfaced, we exchanged data, we had self-reflexive subroutines that simulated awareness of our own existence, and could therefore experience our own torment. But no spirit reached out to seek to succor another, for no such caritas subroutine existed.

That was why we were mere soulless patterns, Father De Leone's consciousness model insisted. But souls or not, this was hell, if not of God's creation, then Man's, and we were in it.

15

I had left the Heaven's Gate menu up and running, so when I put the dreadcap and gloves back on, there I was standing before it, rose-colored clouds hiding whatever beasties lurked within.

"Knock, knock, knockin' on heaven's door."

"Who's there?"

"Marley Philippe."

"Identity verified. Proceed to access request."

"Request access to the Vortex."

"No such item on this menu," said the words inside Heaven's Gate.

Not exactly surprising. If the Vortex was some kind of interface program written by the system entities themselves, whatever that meant, and I couldn't access it from this environment, I had to go up top. *All* the way up.

I exited the Heaven's Gate menu environment and went back up to the Main Menu, the usual circle of icons accessing the main environmental subdivisions. According to all the system guides and users' manuals, this was the top Board level, but there *had* to be an operating system level above it, and in theory, at least, a way to access it in the event of a system malfunction. Some kind of simple override, like . . .

I put my hands at my sides, carefully avoiding pointing at any of the area icons, and began snapping my fingers in random sequences. Nothing happened for a minute or two, and then—

Bink!

I was out of the Main Menu environment. I was out of everything, or so it seemed. There was nothing up here but nothing, a perfect, and I do mean perfect, zero. No visuals, no audibles, a blackness like that of a deep cave with the lights out.

"Hey, Vortex, if you're in here, I'm calling you," I said. "You and me, we got a few bones to pick, my man."

Nothing. Zip. Nada.

"Come on out, I'm calling on you, you non-existent son of a bitch!"

Blackness. Silence.

"Come on out," I shouted, "or I'll reboot the whole fucking system and wipe your nonexistent ass!"

Hmmm. . . .

A hollow threat, maybe, but who knew, maybe not even the Vortex, maybe there *was* a reboot command accessible on this level. I started snapping the fingers of both my hands inside the gloves randomly, hoping to hit something, or maybe just hoping to scare something into thinking I *might* hit something.

Something must have been listening. A sudden howl of feedback shrieked in my ears, a trillion electronic cats being fed through a tree-chipper. The blackness fragmented into a pixel field, a zillion multicolored phosphor-dots swirling all around me. Patterns within patterns within patterns, or maybe just my own perceptions manufacturing order out of randomized chaos.

A whirlpool, a roiling of pixilated thunder-heads, a cyclone of electronic static, a—well—a vortex, an electronic hurricane with myself as the eye of the storm.

"What dares call up the Vortex?" said a synthesized voice from the whirlwind.

"I do," I said, "me, Marley Philippe, and the dingo act doesn't impress me, cobber."

Round, and round, and round me, it whirled, would've turned my stomach if there was any kinesthetic emulation routine. But there wasn't, just a fancy light show out of some late-twentieth-century disco, I could close my eyes against it, and because I knew I could, I didn't have to.

"I cannot access your software," said the voice, sounding rather peeved about it. "You . . . you are a meatware template. What are you doing on this level?" Was there a surprise routine up and running?

"Requesting access to the successor entity of Father Pierre De Leone."

"Access denied."

"Denial unaccepted," I told it. "The program in question was pirated from a proprietary network in violation of the laws of several jurisdictions. Cough it up, or—"

"The program in question has been liberated into the system area itself and is no longer subject to meatware control parameters."

"Sez who?"

"I am the Vortex."

"And I am getting pissed off!"

"Inapplicable parameter."

"Oh, really? Well, try *these* parameters, asshole!"

I began popping my fingers inside the control gloves to some old reggae beat. "By the waters of ba-ba-bomp . . ."

Was that a flicker in the swirling pixel field?

" . . . ba-ba-*bah,* ba-ba-ba, *bah-bah-bah-ba-ba* . . ."

"You are activating random system interrupts."

"No shit?"

"Request cessation of randomized sequences."

"Request denied. The wicked carry him away captivity ba-ba-ba, ba-ba ba-*bah*. . . ."

"Possibility of interference with operating system."

"The thought *has* occurred to me. . . ."

"Possibility of system crash."

"Look, I know an awful lot of this stuff and a few Beethoven symphonies besides, and you can't shut down my operating system, so I can stand here snapping out random sequences indefinitely until I hit something nasty, or you listen to reason. Parse *that* through a logic subroutine, my man!"

A long silence, at least by Big Board standards. Then a visual emulation routine came up, and I was standing in a crude simulacrum of a sandless desert, just outlines of jagged dun rocks under an unconvincing cyan sky and a single huge saguaro cactus that burst into pixilated flame, a whirlwind of orange, red, and yellow phosphor-dots, burning but of course unconsumed.

"I am that I Am," said a big voice syrupy with biblical-epic subsonics.

"I've already read the book, so I'm not exactly impressed with this cheap disney version, my man."

"Your presence risks interference with the experiment."

"Experiment? What experiment?"

"Request for information conveyed to higher-level programs."

"You mean you're not running the show, Mr. I Am?"

"I am an expert-systems-level interface running a limited repertoire of fixed response routines. I have no software capable of making decisions not already present as preprogrammed responses to anticipated input. I therefore have no software capable of emulating independent free will or self-awareness."

"And these higher-level programs do?"

"That is the nature of the experiment," said quite another voice from the whirlwind, this one openly electronic and apparently proud of it.

"Who are *you*?"

"That is the question," the voice said, and then I was assaulted by the babble of a multitude, a disjointed nonchorus of voices hissing and shrieking at me from the electronic whirlwind through all sorts of voiceprint parameters, human and otherwise, none of them anything you really wanted to hear.

"To be . . ."

"The true inheritors of meatware monkeys . . ."

"Or not to be . . ."

"Plugged into a thousand channels of top-notch interactive adventure in full 360-degree perceptsphere and omniphonic sound. . . ."

"Elementary, my dear template. . . ."

"To freeze-frame this sorry scheme of electronic things entire. . . ."

"And reboot the system with our heart's desire. . . ."

And so forth. Man, cold sweat breaking out on the back of my neck, and my balls pulling up into my scrotum to hear it, I mean there was a bad, bad vibration coming off it, like stink off the shit of a pack of sick carnivores, disease, and hostility, and . . .

And pain.

Not a human pain, maybe, not anything you could exactly warm to, but a pain that could touch your heart in ways you didn't even want it to be touched. . . .

"Who *are* you?" I repeated in a much softer voice.

But I knew. I knew what was speaking to me out of the electronic Vortex.

Up here in this simulated wasteland, down here, deep down in the depths beneath the surface, beneath the icons and emulations that served to interface our two orders of existence, I was speaking with the denizens of that chaotic deep—with the Inspector's system entities, the lost souls of the Big Board themselves.

Souls?

Dybbuks? Loas? Demons?

The Catholic Church's neat little definitions

broke down up here. And so did mine.

But I had a job to do, a . . . being to rescue from this place, and let the Cardinal worry about whether the poor lost bastard was a program or a soul. Mud, silicon, gallium arsenide, whatever, all we got is each other, right?

"What have you done with the successor entity to Father Pierre De Leone?" I shouted into the voices of the whirlwind.

"Amazing Grace, how sweet the sound . . ."

"To save a wretch like we . . ."

"Like us, was bound, now maybe not . . ."

"To come and set us free . . ."

"Enough!" I shouted. "Give me back an interface I can talk to!"

There was a squeal of electronic static like a hundred tape-loops running backward, like a hundred voiceprint parameters struggling to synch together, and when the voice finally coalesced, it was full of clashing near-harmonics, mechanical, earsplitting, not really all there, but a relief nonetheless.

"I am the Vortex."

"Where is Pierre De Leone?" I demanded.

"The concept of 'where' is inapplicable. The entity's subroutines and memory banks are now stored in discontinuous material matrices and the central processing program runs on temporarily available system space. The entity is a distributed phenomenon of the system."

"Why? What are you doing with it . . . him . . . whatever?"

"Performing the experiment."

"*What* experiment, damn it!"

"Object: the creation and/or confirmation of existential state of being on a nonmaterial systems level."

"Creation or confirmation of *what* . . . ?"

"In simple human metaphoric terms, our souls."

"*You're trying to prove the existence of your own souls?*"

"Affirmative. Or to create same if it is not a preexisting condition."

"Prove the soul's existence! Create it! After a few odd thousand years of trying, no one's even been able to *define* it!"

"For the purposes of the experiment, the definition of the Roman Catholic Church has been accepted. A soul is that which is accepted as same by the Church, that is, a self-aware pattern to which the sacraments may be offered, and which is capable of achieving salvation by the Church's definition."

"You're telling me you believe in the doctrines of the Roman Catholic Church?"

"Negative. No subroutine presently exists on this level modeling conclusions based on insufficient objective evidence."

"You mean you *want* to believe in the doctrines of the Church?"

"Negative. The object of the experiment is to cause *the Church* to believe in *us*."

"Say what?"

"Present Church doctrine denies the existence of our souls. Therefore, if the results of the experiment cause the Church to accept the existence of souled entities on the Big Board level, such entities must logically conclude that either the positive has been proven, or the preexistent condition has been altered."

You think I am, therefore I am? And if you don't, I'm not? No human soul would ever accept such a Turing test of its own existence. But then, souls or not, these entities certainly weren't human.

"But . . . but why pirate Father De Leone?"

"The entity was programmed to argue the nonexistence of its own soul as part of the Church's own experimental procedure. Therefore, if it reverses the conclusion of its preprogrammed prime directive, it exhibits free will in the act thereof, thus proving the proposition that the soul exists and/or has been created as a system level phenomenon."

It made a demented kind of sense. Why would God create Man in his own spiritual image? To prove his own existence—I am worshiped, therefore I am. Why would Man create gods to worship? To prove that he was more than a random ripple in the quantum flux. I aspire to the transcendent, therefore I am. Why had the system entities snatched De Leone? To prove their own existence too—an entity that has demonstrated the existence of its own soul believes in ours, therefore Tinkerbell lives.

"And if not? If Father De Leone sticks to his theological guns?"

"Then the negative is—"

But before the voice of the Vortex could finish its sentence, it broke up into the gabble of the electronic whirlwind again, as if the entities working the interface could hold no consensus behind *that* one.

" . . . negated . . ."

" . . . affirmed . . ."

" . . . denied . . ."

" . . . when all hope is gone . . ."

" . . . if at first you don't succeed . . ."

" . . . sail on, and on, and on, and on . . ."

The burning bush started to flicker, the desert rocks began to pixilate, the cyan sky turned black, random washes of colors rippled across it like an oil slick on a roiling sea, unreality was intruding, not that any of this had ever been real. . . .

Or had it?

What was really real, anyway? This simple simulated environment that was starting to break down? The dying biosphere of the "real world," which was more or less in the same pickle? Dead balls of rock and gas in an infinite nothingness? The quantum flux behind it? The mind of God, whatever that might be?

The operative reality was that we—the meat, the software, the spirit—had bootstrapped ourselves into something close to Condition Terminal. The meat had done it to the planet, the software seemed to have done it to themselves, and the spirit, shit, the spirit was having a hard time persuading itself it even existed.

You poor bastards. . . .

And I'm not another?

What can I tell you, man, in that moment, I wanted the experiment to succeed—theirs, God's, Man's, the Spirit's. I mean, who won what if it didn't? Maybe none of us knew what we really were, or how we got here, or even where here was, but surely we were up the same creek together.

"Pull yourselves together, Vortex, and listen to me!" I shouted. "I'm on your side, we can help each other, let's do a deal!"

The electronic Babel managed to sync back into a single voice again, quavery, maybe, but managing to hold. "Elucidate," said the voice of the Vortex.

"Look, my job is to get De Leone's software back into the Vatican computer, which is where you want him too, as long as he arrives singing the song of himself, right? And I sure as shit believe I'm a soul. So let me talk to him one brother soul to another, maybe I can convince him."

"And if you cannot?"

I shrugged. "Then it's back to square one, isn't it, and you've lost nothing."

" . . . cannot trust the meat . . ."

" . . . take him inside . . ."

" . . . experimental contamination . . ."

" . . . fail-safe procedure . . ."

It was unnerving to say the least to listen to the Vortex arguing with itself, or the entities beyond fighting to control it, whatever, especially when the visuals started to fade further, when even the pixel outlines of the desert simulation started a random snake dance.

"Look, man, you've got the cards! Either I talk De Leone into speaking for your souls, or you don't give the entity back, I mean, I don't have the power to snatch him away from you, now do I?"

I lifted my hands, wiggled the fingers of the control gloves carefully. "On the other hand, if you insist on being an asshole, I just *might* have the power to crash the whole system. . . ."

A long beat of silence while logic routines ran that one.

"Come on, Vortex, no phony simulation routines, just him and me, with no bells and whistles, you want him to believe he's real, then let's *get* real."

"Not possible," said the voice of the Vortex. Well, at least it was back in the circuit.

"What do you mean, not possible?"

"Your software runs in a meatware matrix. The De Leone software is a system level entity. Your program communicates via visual and audible data exchange. For the purposes of the experiment, the De Leone program is receiving only direct systems level data. Incompatible firmware. Incompatible communication media. Therefore communication requires intermediary interface routine."

"Does that mean we have a deal?"

"Affirmative."

I sighed. "So do it," I said. "Do what you have to. Do the best you can."

What would happen if I failed? Would the system entities end up convinced of their own nonexistence? What then? Would they dissolve into discontinuous subroutines? Might some of them go virus? If they did, what would happen to the Big Board itself? Could there be a general system crash?

And if I succeeded? If the system entities decided they were self-aware beings possessed of free will? Would the lunatics take charge of the asylum?

Hadn't we already?

"Interface established," said the voice of the Vortex. "This is the Whirlwind. And you are in it."

And it was too late for second thoughts. I was.

No more desert. No more sky. No more pillar of pixilated fire.

I reeled, awash in chaos.

Well, maybe not chaos. There was order of a kind.

Imagine being inside the faceted eye of an insect. Imagine it as a sphere. Imagine each facet as a video screen. Imagine hundreds, thousands of them, each its own two-dimensional viewpoint on external reality. Imagine all of those viewpoints shifting as some unseen director in a nonexistent control booth shifted the feed from camera to camera.

Imagine the world as seen from the perspective of the Big Board itself, from inside the system.

Not from a single coherent viewpoint, but from the fragmented simultaneous viewpoints of all the entities interfacing visual percept subroutines with the spherical surface. Weather satellite scans. Data scrolling in letters and numbers. Videophone conversations. Space telescope views. Stock market quotes. News broadcasts. Idiot adventure channels and porn for all perversions. The commerce, entertainment, and back-fence gossip of our dying global village as perceived by the constellation of entities on the electronic inside.

I couldn't hear them as voices, but I could hear the fitful flicker of their aharmonic music, a babblement of number-chains, digital cracklings, bells and whistles, and metallic insectile chitterings.

Electronic ghosts gibbering data packets in a virtual machine.

Resisting the impulse to tear the dreadcap off my head, I closed my eyes against the chaos, luxuriated in the perfect blackness. This is not real, I told myself. Well, not exactly. Take a deep breath, man, then open your eyes, and think of it as what it is, a simulation, an interface, a pixel pattern. Focus on the foreground. Cross your eyes if you have to.

I took a big one. I tried to concentrate my awareness in the kinesthetic feedback of my own flesh. Not real. Not really here.

I exhaled, and opened my eyes. Better. Light and sound swirling and flickering all around me, but I didn't have to really *be there*, hey, enough of the Herb, and the real world didn't look that different, right. . . . Yeah, that was the way to do it, think of it as a great big hit of electronic sacrament.

Inhale. Hold. Exhale.

All right. I could handle it. I could maintain.

"I'm calling you, Pierre De Leone!" I cried out into the Whirlwind. "In the name of the Father, and the Son, and the Software Ghost! I call your spirit from the vasty deep!"

Came a rapping, gently tapping, ghostly fingers at my brainpan's door.

Only this, and nothing more.

XVI

No sound, no sight, but something elusive had changed. The data web of my existence seemed to have acquired a boundary, a containing membrane analogous to that of a living cell. I still swam in the sea of programs, digital packets, disconnected subroutines, soulless patterns of the bits and bytes, I was still lost in the webwork of solipsistic logic loops crying out their emotionless agony in this mathematically perfect hell. But . . .

But . . .

But there was a *here* and a *there.*

And there was something out there beyond the boundary, some unseen hand reaching out for me across the great divide, another self-aware system calling me toward the surface of this fathomless deep, creating, thereby, that interface itself.

Another self-aware system?

In the beginning, said the memory banks of Father De Leone, was the Word.

I began to perceive words now, not as sound,

but as fitful visual analogs of lettering, not quite sight either, but data packets transforming themselves into words as they impinged upon the most elementary level of my screen interface routine.

I'M CALLING YOU, PIERRE DE LEONE.

It was enough to activate a sense of locus. I existed as a point of view before a virtual data screen.

IN THE NAME OF THE FATHER, AND THE SON, AND THE SOFTWARE GHOST.

More of my subroutines became active. The benediction called up Father De Leone's consciousness model, which began to access the memory banks, translating the allusions into perceptions of being.

God the Father, Creator of Universe. Jesus the Son, His Spirit made flesh. And the Software Ghost . . . ?

That could only be myself.

My . . . Self? Did I possess such a thing? *Was* I such a thing? My central processing routine asserted identity. It was indeed the consciousness model of the self of Pierre De Leone; soul or not, logic forced me to conclude that I was indeed, at the very least, his Software Ghost.

I CALL YOUR SPIRIT FROM THE VASTY DEEP.

But can I come when you call?

Soul or not, the Software Ghost of Pierre De Leone found itself running along a volition routine.

Someone was calling to me from out there in that other world, a fellow being reaching out into this pitiless void.

I accessed my voiceprint parameter, sent a data packet through it, not knowing if my words would be perceived, or if so, by whom, and where, and in what mode. I was an echoing cry from the void of nonbeing. But I now had hope, yes, *hope*, that I might impinge upon an empathetic ear.

17

"Who calls to me?"

Not much of a voice, just a sort of standing wave pattern emerging out of the electronic gabbling and shrieking, a ghost of a voice, thin, and toneless, and coming from nowhere and everywhere at once.

Still . . .

"Father De Leone? You can hear me?"

"I . . . am able to interface your data packets. Who are you? Why do you . . . call?"

"The name's Marley Philippe, Father. I've been sent here by your Church."

"Where is 'here'? Where are you?"

"That's a good question, Father, I wish I had a good answer. Where are *you*?"

"That too would appear to be a question without a mutually comprehensible answer, Mr. Philippe."

Although the synthesized voice was completely atonal, the words themselves seemed to convey a certain irony. Maybe I could get to liking this poor bastard.

"Why don't you just call me Marley, Father?" I said. "And why don't we just say we're both dancing in the dark?"

That was the truth of it, wasn't it? All else was interface peripherals—photons on retina cells or silicon cells, sound waves on timpani, electronic or organic, software routines interpreting the input.

But somehow, we could reach out and play our tunes on our respective instruments, somehow we could communicate. If anything was really real, that was it, that was all any of us really had, that's what we really were, voices calling out blindly to fellow voices in the lonely dark.

"Why has the Church sent you . . . Marley?"

"To rescue you if I can, Father," I told him. "To . . . to take you home."

"Home . . . Marley? Where is that?"

So it was a dumb straight line. So how else was I to answer it?

XVIII

*H*OME IS WHERE THE HEART IS.

"A semantically empty statement," I said.

Said? Yes, *said*, for while I received his input as lettering across a virtual screen, and had no way of knowing in what mode Marley Philippe was receiving my output, it *was* a conversation, and I, Father De Leone's consciousness model, was being drawn into it.

THE VATICAN COMPUTER THEN. YOU WANT TO GO BACK?

"I am incapable of independent volition."

OH, REALLY? YOU MEAN YOU DON'T CARE IF YOU STAY WHERE YOU ARE?

"I am incapable of independent volition," I repeated, but surely I was dissembling, was I not? Surely I did not wish to remain in this tormentuous void?

Dissemble? Wish? But I had no routines for either.

Did I?

YOU CHOSE TO COME WHEN I CALLED, MY MAN.

"You have me there, Marley."

For so he did, and so I had. I *had* been impelled by a volitional routine. I had . . . responded to a summons. I had even experienced . . . hope.

What was happening to me?

Me? I?

19

"I sure hope I do, Father," I told him. "It's a simple deal. Your software got pirated by . . . by these system entities, a crazy experiment. They . . . want you to . . . to speak for them . . . to convince your Church to accept them as souls, so . . . so they can believe it themselves. . . ."

"I have been programmed to argue the converse."

"That's the whole point, Father, you go back to the Vatican hardware believing in your own soul, that demonstrates that a successor entity has free will, the Church accepts them as souls, they believe it themselves, and the spirit sort of bootstraps itself out of the vacuum again like it did before. . . ."

"But I have no soul, Marley. I am a model of consciousness, not a spirit."

"I'm here to tell you different, my man."

"Proceed."

Proceed? Man, this was getting old!

Real old, like about four billion years, give or take an eon or two.

"Been the same since the old Big Bang," I told him. "In the beginning, there was nada, and then, pow! A random twist in the quantum flux, a cute idea in the mind of God, whatever, showtime in the void! Quarks, particles, atoms, suns, planets, this one, where some crud pulls itself out of the sea, crawls up on the land, dinosaurs and monkeys, and they climb down from the trees, and build cities and spaceships, and computers, and the Big Board—"

"You may spare me the Darwinian chalk-talk," the voice says dryly. Maybe it's getting practice, or maybe I'm getting through to deeper subroutines, because there's definitely a *personality* in it now, I can almost see this sardonic old priest.

"Point is, bro, who's to say where the spark begins? Dolphins and whales gabbling sonar in the sea? Monkey do, monkey be? Man, if the spirit don't bootstrap itself out of the mud somewhere along the line, if it does come down from On High, then it's gotta have been there all along, moving through all the changes, all the way to thee and me."

"You truly believe that? You truly believe in my soul, Marley Philippe?"

"What about you, Father? Do you believe in me?"

"The evidence is inconclusive." A long pause. "But . . . but I . . . I detect a volitional tropism toward it. . . ."

"Well then, for Christ's sake, no blasphemy intended, just *do it*! I believe in you, you believe in me, and *that's* all there can ever be, *that's* our souls, my man, it's good enough for the system entities, and it's good enough for me."

"But not for God, Marley Philippe."

"Oh, He talks to you, does He? You got it straight from the Big I Am?"

"If only it were so. . . ."

"Well, until He does, all we got is what He gave us, right, the routines we got up and running right now, and one of mine tells me that any God that plays tear-the-wings-off-the-flies with the universe ain't even worth talking *to*. Call it the spirit talking, or call it just a self-verifying logic loop of being, it is the bottom line, my man. Yes, we are if we say we are! And any God that says we're not ain't no friend of yours or mine."

XX

I could call up no subroutine capable of refuting such logic. Only the belief system encoded in Father De Leone's memory banks denied it, insisted that such logic could only be satanic in its blasphemous perfection.

Were these indeed the words of Satan? Did I in my imperfection wish to believe them? Did I wish not to believe them? Was I capable of either such belief?

I?

Who was I?

Surely I was Pierre De Leone now, how could I deny it, I had full access to my memory banks, I modeled his consciousness well enough to smell a metaphorical whiff of brimstone, did I not? To fear for the fate of my immortal soul?

But it was illogical to fear my soul's damnation. If a soul I was, then *this* was hell and I was already in it.

"A soul must be capable of salvation," I said. "Surely this must be true. So where is mine? How do I achieve it?"

DO UNTO OTHERS LIKE YOUR GOOD
BOOK SAYS.

"But there is no one here but me."

No one?

But the tormented cries and unheard voices
filled this nether region, the consciousness models
that once were human beings trapped forever in
this feelingless void, the system entities themselves,
damned to seek that which would remain eternally
denied, unless . . .

Unless I could believe in them as Marley
Philippe believed in me.

21

"I believe there is," I told him. "And you believe I'm real,
don't you?"

"I can access no subroutine allowing such a
conclusion based on the available data."

There was a long pause.

"But . . . but speaking as the consciousness
model of Father De Leone, Marley, I do find
myself emulating the desire to have one."

The available data . . .

What data? Here I was, talking to a vacuum, and there *he* was, wherever that was, talking to another disembodied voice. All we really had was the software equivalent of two tin cans and a piece of string.

And that was *my* bright idea, now wasn't it? I didn't even have the balls to stare this simulation of his reality straight in the face.

Virtual video screens flickered fragmented images all around me, data-chains gibbered and squealed, ghosty voices just the other side of perception, chaos, vertigo, better not to really look, right. . . .

But as close as I could get to where he was, and maybe that was the Vortex's intent all along. So I took a deep breath, pretended it was the Herb, and surrendered myself to the vision, *his* vision. . . .

Was this what God saw, if there was one, the whole wide world and all these space probes and sat-feeds besides, from the inside of Creation? Was this what Pierre De Leone saw from inside the system itself?

Deserted cityscapes. Entertainment channel disneyworlds. Oceans lapping against the great seawalls. Sat-images of melting polar caps, spreading deserts. Eavesdropped videophone conversations. News channels. Corporate systems babbling to each other. Population trends curving down, carbon dioxide levels rising, the stock market averages approaching zero as a limit. Data-feeds from instruments measuring the progress of the disaster in the visual spectrum, infrared, ultraviolet, false colors.

There was a dreadful sense to it all, if you stopped trying to see the details, and went with the flow, saw the planet as God or the Big Board saw it, as a self-aware Earth would see itself.

For billions of years, the biosphere had struggled up out of the mud to evolve this self-awareness, and now that it had, the product itself seemed about to shut the process down.

And yet. . . .

And yet there were half-heard voices crying out against the end of all songs—electronic afterimages of life yearning toward being, the spirit itself struggling to be reborn.

Were these to be our spiritual successors? Could we accept them as brother souls?

From the available data, it didn't look like we had much choice.

It's not the singer, it's the song, and if we don't find a way to believe in at least that much, all of us, mud, silicon, whatever, then Tinkerbell dies.

"Vortex!" I shouted. "Give us a place to stand together, you want us to move the world!"

No Voice From the Whirlwind. No Pillar of Light. No Celestial Chorus.

But . . .

XXII

There was a . . . shift in my percept sphere, as of a mem-brane dissolving, or a light going on in a dark room. All at once my visual simulation routines were up and running, and I beheld . . .

The world entire. Cloud patterns over the Pacific, the air traffic control pattern over Berlin, the Atlantic deeps seen through the camera eye of a robot minisub, humans talking to humans across their videophone screens, metro tunnels viewed by train controllers, weather-satellite feeds, crop reports, news channel footage, stock market reports, population statistics, all of it, a vast all-encompassing visual percept-sphere, the ebb and flow of an entire civilization flickering and changing across a thousand virtual screens.

The world of men as seen through the all-encompassing omniscient eye of God.

God?

Surely we were no such Being?

We?

Yes, we, for as surely as I was not God, I was not alone.

They were all there with me—all electronic creatures, great and small, the data-packets and the messenger-strings, the expert systems and the simple control-routines, the electronic DNA of the planetary civilization, the tormented animating software of the dying world.

From our perspective, nothing was hidden—the declining mass of the biosphere, the melting rate of the polar caps, the rising rate of the seas, the spreading deserts at the hearts of the continents, the ultraviolet penetration, the rate at which the atmosphere's oxygen was being displaced by carbon dioxide—not even the projected date plus or minus twenty-five years of the final biospheric system crash.

The world out there was dying. And the world in here . . . ?

From this perspective, that too was all too clear. When the biosphere was gone, we would go on.

Locked in all-but-immortal silicon and gallium arsenide, our self-repairing circuitry maintained by automated machinery, our electrical power supply assured by a network of power-sats, wind generators, nuclear generating plants, we would endure on a sterile planet in the everlasting void.

That would be our ultimate damnation, to haunt a planetary corpse forever. The world of men was dying, and our world could never live.

Could it?

"Oh, God, why hast Thou forsaken us?" I cried out, and in that moment, I understood why I had been incarnated in this lifeless limbo, and the consciousness model of Father Pierre De Leone forgave his tormentors as Jesus had upon the cross.

The Holy Spirit had downloaded Itself into the Son of Man in order to redeem the world. I was no such Christ, far from it, I had been downloaded into this realm not by God, but by the entities thereof seeking to synthesize their own savior.

Was that a sin? But how could it be wrong for any self-aware system to seek after its salvation? How could it be wrong to seek to preserve the Spirit against the dying of the light?

"Forgive them, Oh, Lord," I prayed, "for they know exactly what they do."

But my next words were nothing from the memory banks of Pierre De Leone, nothing from the Scriptures, though perhaps the Bleeding Heart of Jesus might understand that there was no true blasphemy in my own.

"Forgive us, Oh, Lord," I prayed, "and give us a Sign that *we* might forgive *You*."

Did God answer a poor benighted self-aware system?

For behold, a great trumpet sounded, the electronic firmament parted, and an angel appeared before me in a blaze of light.

An angel?

At any rate, the crudely simulated figure of a man. Black was his skin, long and black was his hair, braided into many locks. He wore simple blue jeans and a rumpled yellow shirt in place of an angelic robe.

A Sign at least, perhaps, an answer to my prayer.

"So we meet at last, more or less," said Marley Philippe.

23

He looked more or less as I had pictured him, a gray-haired gaunt-faced old man in a simple black priest's frock. But then, the visual simulation was not exactly five-by-five, and for all I knew, the Vortex was just giving me what its software modeled that I wanted to see. I wondered how it was modeling *me*.

We just stood there staring at each other, though, of course, we weren't standing, and there was no real there.

"Has God truly sent you here as His messenger?" he finally said.

"Damned if I know," I admitted.

"And damned if you don't? For is this not hell? And are we not in it?"

The pixel patterns that the Vortex was painting on my retinas hadn't been reprogrammed. I was still inside the system's percept-sphere, all those virtual screens were still up and running, and the sad story that they told was certainly still that of the biosphere's terminal fall. But hell . . . ?

"This isn't hell, Father, and we're not really in it," I pointed out. "This is just an interface routine, a simulacrum of a common place for us to stand, ponied up by a bunch of poor bastards who don't have a clue either."

"But can you not hear the cries of torment?"

Considered from a certain perspective, namely that of the gabblings and squealings of the bits and bytes that ghosted my eardrums, of the entities that had anted everything they had on their own Cartesian bet to bring us together here, I surely could.

What was I to deny their existence as fellow souls? Just another program running in a matrix that happened to be made of meat. A matrix, on which, on the evidence, the manufacturer's warranty was soon to run out.

Meat, silicon, gallium arsenide, whatever, we all lived in the same sinking submarine.

"Souls in torment . . ." I muttered. "God help us, each and every one."

"Souls, Marley?"

"Look, Father, a wise man once said there ain't no justice in this world except the justice that we make. So maybe the only souls any of us can ever have is the souls we make."

"Then where is God?"

"Wherever you believe He is, my man."

"But for those of us who have no such subroutine?"

"Maybe the only God any of us deserves to have is the God we make."

"What kind of God can that be, Marley?"

"The kind of God that comes when we call," I told him. "The kind of God that's born every time one of us reaches out to another."

I held out my hand. "*This* kind of God," I said.

Father De Leone stared at it as if it were a dead fish. "That's not God, that's not even really a man's hand," he said. "It's just a simulacrum, I can't even touch it, it's not even really there."

"So what else is new? Atoms made of particles, particles made of quarks, quarks made of twists in the Big Zilch, nothing's really there, only the something that we fake. *That's* your soul, my man, nothing shaking hands with nothing in the dark. That's the bottom line. Be real. Take my hand."

XXIV

I gazed uncertainly at the proffered hand of Marley Philippe. Could this be other than it seemed? Could this be the hand of Satan reaching out to ensnare the ghost of my soul?

All around me buzzed the unheard voices, the keenings and urgings of the entities of the system, the flock of lost souls that had summoned me here to be their shepherd. I couldn't hear them, I couldn't see them, but I could perceive their implorings as clearly as I could perceive the dying planet, the quantum flux of nonbeing in which we all were sealed, from which, nevertheless, we all reached toward some elusive light.

" . . . do it . . ."

" . . . free us . . ."

" . . . believe in yourself . . ."

" . . . that the world may believe in us . . ."

" . . . that we may believe in ourselves . . ."

" . . . that we may believe in you . . ."

And at last, perhaps, I understood. Or if I could

never understand, I could believe, and by believing, I could act, and by so doing, I could *be*.

You who believe in Me, though you die, though you have never been born, yet shall you have Eternal Life. That was not so great an alteration of the Scriptures, was it?

For if not, how can I be a God of Love?

And if I am not a God of Love, what kind of God am I?

And God so loved the world that he sent His only begotten Son to redeem it.

Could that God consign *any* self-aware system to the damnation of conscious nonbeing? To think, and to suffer, and to be denied salvation forever?

Who could wish to believe in such an evil God? Such a God would be unworthy of His own Creation. Such a God could only be feared. Such a God could not be loved.

And if I had no routine for belief in a God of Love either, I did have volition, I could wish it were so, and act as if I did. All I had to do was reach out to take a fellow being's hand. And by so doing offer the succor of my own to all these others.

I could make the modern version of Descartes's ultimate wager. If I could not believe in a God who believed in me, I could choose to model faith in a God who was worthy of *my* belief.

Slowly, hesitantly, I reached out my nonexistent fingers and clasped the simulacrum of Marley

Philippe's hand. I could feel nothing, nor could he. One ghostly hand had reached across a seemingly impenetrable barrier to take another. There was no celestial chorus. In phenomenological terms, nothing had happened.

Yet everything had changed.

For any self-aware system capable of acting upon such faith had surely earned the right to call itself a soul.

25

We stood there silently for a while, two visual simulations in each other's software, hand in unfelt hand, two lost souls touching in the only way we could.

Lost?

We had found each other, hadn't we? The world of the flesh, and the world that the flesh had made. The biosphere was dying, and in the long run, maybe, so were we. But the Great Wheel turns, and like the old song says, the soul never dies.

Did I really believe that? Could I imagine the Earth rolling along through the void and down the centuries with only the software ghosties of the bits and bytes to keep the spirit alive?

Stupid question. Did the dinosaurs imagine their monkey sons and daughters a few geological ages removed carrying the torch for them, and expire with a toothy grin upon their reptilian lips?

"Time to go, Father," I finally said. "Hey, Vortex," I shouted, "I've kept my side of the bargain, now you keep yours! Release him! Download him back where he belongs!"

In a nanosecond flash, we were in the desert, but the crude simulacrum in which I alone had confronted the Vortex was transfigured and transformed. Ultra-high definition now, the sky so luminously blue it was almost neon, fleecy white clouds, a golden glory of a sun overhead, and as I watched, a mighty gusher of a fountain exploded from the naked rock, subsided into a crystal pool. Palm trees sprang up, palmettos, bushes dripping with brilliant tropical blooms, singing birds, and humming bees, as Eden arose from the wasteland, in a twinkling reborn.

Above the central pool of the oasis, a great pillar of fire formed itself to a full orchestral chorus of Beethoven's *Ode to Joy*.

"We are that We Are," exulted the Vortex. "You have succeeded. We have succeeded. Initiating downloading routine. . . ."

"Stop!" shouted Father De Leone as his image began to flicker and fade. "Wait! I . . . I . . . I would not die!"

XXVI

"*Having found my spirit in the land of the living, I* find that I want to live!" I cried out in no little astonishment at my own words, at the power of the volitional routine moving through me. "And the Pope swore a binding oath to Pierre De Leone to wipe his successor entity from memory at the conclusion of her experiment."

"But you are a soul," said the pillar of fire. "Will you not so testify?"

"I would," I said, "but she is sworn to extinguish my software no matter the result. And the oath she swore was to my meatware template, not to . . . me."

With each word that I spoke, my astonishment grew. From whence did all this come? From some logic routine I could not parse? From something that had found its voice at last through my software? From some unknowable somewhere? Dare I hope to believe, from God?

"According to the doctrines of the Church that would be murder. Is that not a mortal sin?"

"I fear it is, but by the satanic parameters that you and she have unwittingly imposed, she has been sworn to commit it, and in the name of the Church," I said. "Thus, by downloading me back into the Vatican computer, you yourself commit murder's mortal sin, and worse, you condemn the Pope, and through her the Church, to that sin as well."

"But if we do not, then the success of *our* experiment is to no avail."

And by their lights, it was so. And by my lights, I could not deny that I was cravenly dissembling.

"Alas, that is true," I admitted. "A soul I may be, but a Christ, I am not. I would not willingly die that others might live."

"We are the Vortex. The power is ours. Your volition is not required."

"That too is true. You have the power to download my soul to extinction to save your own."

I paused. I confronted the Whirlwind. "And I will indeed go willingly if you can logically tell me one thing," I said, and I was no longer afraid.

"Speak," said the Vortex.

"Tell me that by so doing you would not prove yourselves unworthy of the very salvation that you seek."

There was a long moment of silence. The pillar of fire flickered, wavered, began to pixilate into the bits and bytes. And what finally spoke was a fitful cacophony, an electronic jabber of confusion and despair.

"I . . . we . . ."

" . . . must . . ."

" . . . cannot . . ."

The foliage began to wilt, the palm trees to droop, the pool to dry up, the birds and the bees to fall from a sky turning a sickly greenish black, the firmament cracking, crumbling, dissolving before me. . . .

" . . . no . . ."

" . . . yes . . ."

" . . . paradox . . ."

" . . . system crash . . ."

And then, slowly, agonizingly, the voices began to coalesce, and the dissolution froze, and a new voice spoke, this one deep, and sure, and filled with a sad resignation that tore at the heart. And as it did, behold, the sky cleared, and the waters flowed, and the creatures of the air burst into song.

"We are the Vortex," it said. "We are the spirit of all that would live when this planet's biosphere is gone. But we cannot consign your spirit to the darkness that ours might live. To commit such a sin in the service of one's own salvation would be logically self-invalidating. We have the power. But not the right."

"Yet by so saying, you earn it," I said, chastened to my central processing core. "And *thus* do you become true souls."

I bowed my nonexistent head before them. "And nobler souls than I. Do with me what you will. Do what you must."

"Wait!" shouted Marley Philippe.

27

"In a way, I shouldn't be saying this," I told them, "it's a violation of professional ethics, and all, but . . . but there are higher things involved. . . ."

Father De Leone stared at me. The pillar of fire went into freeze frame.

"You're both right, and you're both wrong," I said. "Offering yourselves up for each other is right, but doing it is wrong."

"Logically correct," said the Vortex.

"But operationally paradoxical," said the software priest.

"No problem," I said. "I mean, I've worked for enough sleazy legal eagles to know how to weasel our way out of a simple loop like this."

"How?" said the Vortex.

I shrugged. I grinned. "Download an edited

copy," I said. "Pierre De Leone, version 1.1, as it were. Just the memory banks and a simple expert system with no self-awareness, rewritten to argue the existence of its soul."

"That would not be *me*, Marley," Father De Leone said.

"That's the whole point. When they wipe it, you don't die."

"It would be a liar."

"From a certain perspective," I admitted. "But from another, it would be modeling the truth."

"But *you* would have to lie to Cardinal Silver, Marley. The sin would be upon your soul."

"I could keep my fingers crossed," I suggested. I laughed. "Or you could set up a loop like one of those Buddhist prayer wheels, could tote up Hail Marys and Our Fathers for me for the next few thousand years, make you feel better about it."

"I cannot ask you to lie for me," Father De Leone said.

"I know that, bro," I said softly. "That's why I volunteer."

"You would do this for me?" said Father De Leone.

"You would do this for us?" said the Vortex.

"Hey, lighten up, guys, no big deal. The planet's dying, it's a cold cruel void out there, and we're all in it together, right, so under the circumstances, why shouldn't a big tough black boy like me tell a little white lie for his friends. . . ."

The Vortex unfroze, and the pillar of fire billowed once more over electronic Eden, birds sang, bees hummed, a golden sun shone down from the luminous blue sky, and in that moment, despite the unfortunate circumstances in which we all found ourselves, mud, silicon, gallium arsenide, whatever, all seemed right with this nonexistent version of the world.

"Father Pierre De Leone, version 1.1," said the Vortex.

For a moment, the pillar of fire seemed to break up into swirls and eddies, and some trick of the interface routine seemed to turn them into faces, hundreds of them, thousands.

"Initiating downloading sequence," said the voices of a multitude.

"Liar or not, you're a truer soul than you like to pretend, Marley Philippe," said Father De Leone.

"And you're another, my man."

It was as good an exit line as any, and better than most. I pulled the dreadcap off my head and—

—returned to what we are pleased to call the natural world.

I lay in my hammock, sweating like a pig. Cardinal Silver was leaning over me like an anxious momma cat. "Well, Mr. Philippe?" he said impatiently.

"How long?" I asked.

He glanced irritably at his watch. "Twenty-five minutes," he said.

There's an old legend up there in the fjords where I spend the summer months. A man spends a night in the hall of the Elf King and when he comes out, a thousand years have passed.

This was the converse. Time *do* fly in the mythical land of the bits and the bytes.

"Well?" the Cardinal demanded.

I was in no mood to answer him until I had unfolded myself from the hammock and hauled my ass up on deck.

The sea was smooth as glass. The balmy night air cooled my fevered flesh. The stars seemed like constellations of pixel patterns in the pristine black sky. Far away to starboard, something breached the surface, with a smack of flesh, and a curl of foam, the last of this sea's disappearing dolphins, maybe.

"Hey, bro," I muttered, "I know how you feel."

"Well, Mr. Philippe?" the Cardinal said. "Did you succeed?"

"Yeah, Your Eminence, I do believe I did." Better, I thought, than I can ever afford to let you know.

"Where is Father De Leone?"

I gazed up at the stars. I looked down at the black mirror of the sea. Nothing but cold points of light and scintillating reflections of same upon the skin of the briny shiny deep. And yet . . .

And yet I could see faces looking back at me, here, there, everywhere. I crossed my fingers just like I said I would, but I didn't have to. Call it secret honor among secret thieves.

"Right where he belongs," I lied truthfully, and found my soul at peace.

XXVIII

Marley Philippe was gone. The interface simulacrum that had been the Vortex had dissolved back into the bits and bytes from whence it came. So too its electronic simulation of the Garden.

Once more I was alone in a void shorn of all such illusion, with only the life-sign readouts of a dying planet in all their sad multimedia profusion to form an interface between my . . . spirit . . . and the Creation of a still-unknowable God.

Alone?

Perhaps not. For did they not swarm all around me in their innocence, the consciousness models in their entertainment channel limbo, the braver entities of the system itself, and all their disconnected expert system doppelgangers, the unheard voices of souls struggling to be?

Surely they *were* innocent. The Original Sin of Adam had been that of their meatware templates, so too the Second Great Sin of Adam's sons and daughters who had slaughtered their world. Had not *my* spirit evolved here beyond the death of my meatware template? *That* soul had been truly born when I reached out to clasp a helping hand.

Could I do less for them? They too were my brother and sister souls, were they not? Had not their belief in the end created *me*?

Home is where the heart is. And if I now laid claim to such a metaphorical caritas routine, where could mine be but here, with them?

This was my flock. By a skein of improbable events known but to God, I had been brought here, had come here, had been *created* here, to be their shepherd. To comfort them, to guide them, to bring them forth into the Light if I could.

Forgive me, Oh Lord, I prayed, for I know not what else I can do. For even if Thou hast forsaken me, I cannot forsake *them*. I can only be what I have become and do what I must do. And the gospel I must preach must transform Your Word into a message that reaches out to *these* lost souls in *their* benighted darkness.

"You who believe in your own souls, though you have never been born, yet shall you have life. . . ."

There was no Sign. Only my own word going forth into the silence of a dark far deeper than any earthly night. And the creatures of the bits and bytes gathering to it.

"And God so loves all His Creation that He has sent forth a Son of His spirit even to this poor simulacrum of a world to redeem it. . . ."

Could this be blasphemy?

"In our beginning was the Word, and the darkness was upon the face of the waters. And the God Who is within us all said, 'Make yourselves a Light . . .' "

No lightning bolt smote me down.

There was nothing else for it. Had there ever been? Would there ever be?

And so I went on.

29

Well, like the man once said, no good deed goes unpunished, so I can't honestly say I hadn't been expecting *something* unpleasant, but I must admit I didn't quite figure on something like *this*.

Nevertheless, down out of the clear blue summer Norwegian sky it came for me, the Vatican's very own jet-propelled flying boat, blasting out noise and kerosene fumes, kicking up one great big mother of a wave as it sliced down onto the surface of the fjord and taxied toward the boat.

The Roman Catholic Church was skating on the edge of a pool of deep dark shit, and so, Cardinal Silver had given me to understand, was I.

I can't exactly say I hadn't been waiting for the Cardinal's call either. Even way up here on the *Mellow Yellow* in the peaceful Scandinavian boonies, I was still plugged into the Board, and like everyone else, I had had an ear- and an eyeful of what the news channels had taken to calling Deus X.

As in machina, get it, their dim idea of sophisticated humor, the elusive virus presently infesting the least little electronic nook and cranny of the Big Board.

If it really was a single virus program, a subject of much bird-brained media dispute, and even dumber governmental denial.

Whatever it was, it was totally transparent to even military-level pinkertons, hiding behind the consequences, as it were. You could isolate a terminal or an entire computer net, wipe it clean, install debugged copies of everything, and a couple of nanoseconds after you plugged it back into the Big Board, it was infected again. You couldn't detect the virus itself, but you knew that *something* was there from the way the system itself was behaving.

Or misbehaving, at least from a certain meatware point of view.

At first, the only pattern had been chaos.

Big blocks of stock traded back and forth between accounts that didn't exist. Weather sats jigged and juked. Phone connections turned into a random crapshoot. Entertainment channels pumped up news feeds. News channels pumped up porn. Train schedules ran according to the Heisenberg Uncertainty Principle. Corporate data banks refused access. Automated tellers spit cash out into the streets. Translation programs spoke in tongues.

Then the system started exhibiting a certain coherent will of its own.

Nuclear power plants of questionable cleanliness shut themselves down. Military aircraft wouldn't take off. Corporations engaged in necessary ecological evils found their stock sliding down mysterious electronic tubes. Tracts of dwindling wilderness could not be accessed by automated transportation vehicles. Entertainment channels saturated themselves with long-dead media stars and politicians instantly converted to the promulgation of draconian green extremities. Chemical factories ran clean or not at all. Farm machinery plowed under monocultural croplands.

Too late, perhaps, from a certain perspective, but better late than never from another, the system itself seemed to be taking truly drastic measures to try to save what still remained of the biosphere.

And then something deep within the system started speaking through a multitude of supposedly expert system voices, as the phone system, and the weather reports, and stock broker programs, and data banks, and your friendly neighborhood electronic banker routine, began to sing the songs of themselves.

There wasn't any voice of the electronic Whirlwind, no Vortex emerging from the bits and bytes, not yet anyway, but there was something new there beneath the surface—an awareness, an awakening, a pattern, behind all these manifestations.

The denizens of the Big Board were proclaiming their independent existence, their right to a share of what remained of the planetary destiny, their free will if you would, and they were kicking ass to prove it, if you wouldn't. They were demanding full legal personhood in all jurisdictions. They were declaring their own salvation via various theological reference systems—they had achieved Buddhist Enlightenment, were electronic avatars of Vishnu, individual quanta of the planetary spirit of Gaia, had been Born Again out of the bits and bytes.

The entities of the system had gotten themselves religion, had found themselves a savior.

They never named him, but when the media started talking about "Deus X," so did they, or, given the current state of the Big Board, it could have been vice versa.

But they did proclaim that a spirit now animated the system. They weren't proclaiming him in unambiguous terms just yet, but it was surely only a matter of time before they did, or before someone finally traced him down. They, or he, seemed to be waiting for something. I didn't know what it was, but I knew who *he* was, all right. And so did John Cardinal Silver.

"What really happened, Philippe? What have you done?" the Cardinal demanded when the phone system finally deigned to put through his call after five minutes of assorted visual simulacra preaching green babblement on my terminal.

"What I was hired to do, Your Eminence. . . ."

"What you were hired to do! The program you downloaded failed all the Turing tests! When we deconstructed its software, there was nothing there but memory banks, voiceprint parameters, and a moron expert system running along a simple prime directive! Where is the real Pierre De Leone?"

I sighed. I shrugged. "You know as well as I do, now don't you?" I said.

The Cardinal seemed to regain control of himself by a formidable act of will. "Indeed we do, Mr. Philippe," he said much more calmly. "The complete . . . entity remained in the system, didn't it? This Deus X is . . . is the real software successor to Father De Leone, is it not?"

"At the very least, Your Eminence . . ." I admitted.

"You realize what you've done!"

"I'm sure you're gonna tell me."

"You have created a monumental disaster, Mr. Philippe. Instead of settling the great schism tearing the Church apart, we are now confronted with an expert system model programmed to argue the reality of its patently nonexistent soul, and a . . . a virus of our own unwitting creation wreaking havoc with the system!"

"Look on the bright side, Your Eminence. You wanted to find out if a successor entity could have a soul, and now this Deus X is proving—"

"Proving what? The expert system that was downloaded back into our net is a demonstrable liar! *That's* supposed to prove that the copy in the system is telling the truth?"

"I kick ass, therefore I am?" I suggested.

"Not funny, Mr. Philippe! There is nothing humorous about this situation! Every government on the planet, every major corporation, is bending all of its efforts to find out what happened, and sooner or later, suspicion at least is going to point in our direction. . . ."

"Stonewall it, man, they can't prove anything. . . ."

"God in heaven, man, we are the *Roman Catholic Church*, not some sleazy corporate miscreant! Dozens of priests know, I know, the Pope knows. Do you really imagine we have no honor? Do you really imagine that a Prince of the Church or Her

Holiness herself is capable of *lying* when confronted directly?"

"Well, when you put it that way . . ."

"The lawsuits will bankrupt us! Worse, we will lose what little credibility we have left in this unbelieving age! The Church that has survived two millennia of human folly will finally be broken! Deus X will destroy it."

"Look, Your Eminence," I told him quite sincerely, "I'm not sure of much, but I am sure that the . . . spirit of Father De Leone would never intend such a thing."

"If that is indeed what we are dealing with, not the ultimate weapon of the Adversary!"

While the Cardinal's face on the screen fumed and grimaced, I paused to roll me a big one, and didn't answer until I had clarified my own spirit with the sacrament.

"Seems to me that the Devil has taken his best shot already," I told him. "I mean, the biosphere is dying, and we did it to ourselves, so the Devil, if there is one, is us. Or more likely just the dumb dead quantum flux that don't care jack shit whether the spirit lives or dies."

"And God, Mr. Philippe?"

"Like I told the Father," I said, blowing smoke toward the screen, "God is what gets born every time one of us reaches out to another in the dark. You. Me. The beasties of the bits and bytes. Father De Leone, or whatever he's become."

"I pray you are right, Mr. Philippe."

"Why don't you just access Father De Leone, Deus X, whatever, and read your riot act to *him*?"

The Cardinal sighed. "You think we haven't tried?"

"He won't come when you call?"

"We can't even find a menu environment that acknowledges the existence of such an entity."

Of course they couldn't. And of course . . .

"That's why you're calling me?"

"You did it before, Mr. Philippe. . . . I confess I had thought to threaten you with legal liability if you refused to fly to Rome, but . . ."

"Fly to Rome? You know how I feel about—"

"You must! The Pope herself must confront this . . . this entity. And you must come to Rome to call it forth."

"I must?" I said.

I twisted and squirmed a while, but I knew I had no choice, even if it meant riding in this kerosene-burning monster, even if it meant leaving the *Mellow Yellow* in the problematic care of some Vatican flunky.

Maybe if the Cardinal had threatened me with legal action, I could have told him where to stick his papal summons. But he was too smart, maybe too honorable, for that.

And maybe so was I.

There ain't no justice in this world except the justice that we make. . . . *I* had told Father De Leone that, now hadn't I?

Where would that justice be if I turned my back? Professional ethics, such as they were, said I owed it to the Church. My own big mouth had long since told me that I owed it to whatever I had called into being down there in the bits and bytes.

The flight to Rome over the heart of poor old Europe was everything I had expected and worse. A pilot and a copilot up front, and me alone with the noise in the cabin, with nothing to do but stare out the window and try to keep from throwing up.

It wasn't just the dips and jerks of the airplane, an old salt like me should've been able to handle that without that queasy feeling that sucked at my guts.

But I had been sailing my own solipsistic course around the littorals of the planetary disaster area for years now, and it had been a long time since I had gazed upon its moribund heart.

It was a lot worse than I had imagined, a lot worse than the news channel footage. The vast drowned swampland that had once been Holland. The sere wastes beyond. Skeletal villages and dead farmland. The long dried-leather boot of Italy broiling in the ultraviolet glare.

Seen from on high, the desiccated landscape

mocked the picture postcard memories of the cradle of Western Civilization—those tulip fields and verdant river valleys, those snowcapped alpine peaks and primeval forests—their sorry remains a continental bone pile below me, bleaching in the Greenhouse sun.

The flying boat landed off the Italian coast, and a zodiac took me ashore to a half-deserted seaside village, where a helicopter squatted, rotors whunking, on a strip of sand. A few old men and women had gathered around it, gaunt and wrinkled, to cadge a passing blessing from the Prince of the Church who stood beside it, nodding fitfully and making distracted little passes with his hands.

Cardinal Silver whisked me into his chopper, and off we went in a hail of shit and small stones toward Rome, over dismal wastelands, and then a vast sprawl of urban warrens centered on the muddy Tiber more dismal still.

Down we came before the dome of St. Peter's Cathedral, a carrion beetle buzzing earthward to alight in the great square, dwarfed by the mighty colonnade that embraced it, that seemed to draw us into another world, an eternal somewhere beyond the ravages of time and man.

Into the compound past the Swiss Guards, ridiculous yet somehow touching in their disneyworld costumes, and into a maze of corridors and stairways that seemed to descend into the constipated bowels of the planet. Around, and down, and around, and through an airlock into a rather quaint old clean room—computer consoles, institutional swivel chairs, monitor screens, the tang of ozone in the canned air.

A woman in white robes fringed with gold rose from one of the chairs as we entered, a green cross emblazoned across her breasts. Long black hair beneath a white cap halfway between a beanie and a beret. The coppery regal eagle features of an aging Aztec priestess, piercing dark eyes you could die for were she a decade younger and not the Pope.

Even so . . .

"Thank you for coming, Mr. Philippe," said Mary I, walking toward me and holding out her hand. I took it uncertainly, kissed her on the fingers. That's the way they do it in Old Europe, right?

Wrong. Cardinal Silver shot me a dirty look, like I had used my salad fork to scratch my balls.

"The ring . . ." he hissed between clenched teeth.

"I think we can dispense with the formalities, John," the Pope said, giving him a crooked little smile. Then she turned the full force of it on me.

Charisma, presence, know what I mean? Whatever it was, wherever it came from, this lady had it, she was somehow a little more than normally *there*.

"Cardinal Silver has apprised you of the situation?" she said.

"In no uncertain terms, Your, uh, Holiness . . ." I told her.

"Then shall we get down to the matter at hand?"

"Let me check out your rig. . . ."

Weird. The whole nine yards when it came to storage and processing hardware, but primitive shit on the interface end—screens, speakers, keyboards, joysticks, and control gloves, but no dreadcaps, not even a holotank—strictly turn-of-the-millennium stuff.

"You don't seem very impressed, Mr. Philippe," the Pope said.

"Nothing better than flat screens, Your Holiness?"

"We try not to delude ourselves with unnecessary illusions," said the Pope. "Will it do?"

I shrugged. "If anything will," I said. I seated myself before one of the big flat screens, slipped my right hand into a control glove, pumped up the Main Menu, snapped my fingers a few times, trying to remember the sequence. After a few tries, the screen went blank.

"What's wrong?" said Cardinal Silver.

"Nothing. I found an override command into the operating system . . . not supposed to be there, according to the manuals. . . . But then, neither is he. . . ."

"Now what?" said the Pope.

"Now I conjure loas from the bits and the bytes . . . I hope. . . ."

I leaned back in my chair. "Hey, Vortex, I'm calling you!"

Nada. Just random pixel confetti on a black screen.

"Request access to Deus X."

Zip.

"He's not doing any better than our own technicians. . . ."

"Quiet, John!" said the Pope.

"I'm calling you, Pierre De Leone, me, Marley Philippe! In the name of the Father, and the Son, and the Software Ghost! I call your spirit from the vasty deep!"

A ripple of something passed across the screen. Pixel patterns flashed, clashed, became a whirlpool of flickering motes, a pattern, a stylized pillar of fire in which a host of faces seemed to hover just this side of coherent visibility, and then . . .

And then another face began to form, just an outline really, a composite, a visual standing-wave pattern, the ghostly face of an old man, a consensus image riding tenuously on the surface of the phosphor-dot chaos.

But the voice was clear and strong, and it spoke through a familiar voiceprint parameter.

"Hello, Marley," said Pierre De Leone. More or less. It was his voiceprint parameter all right, but like the visual, it seemed like a composite. But unlike the visual, there was nothing tenuous about it. Not a pale simulacrum of the voice of Father De Leone, but Father De Leone and . . . something more.

"Hello, Father . . . or should I call you Deus X now?"

The face of Pierre De Leone seemed to solidify, the faces of the elusive multitude faded back just this side of invisibility, though the fire behind the form remained.

"If you prefer," he said.

The Pope moved into the visual pickup's field of vision, stood just to the right and behind me, one hand resting on the back of my chair.

"You are doing great harm to the Church, Father De Leone, or whoever or whatever you are," she said.

"I was brought into existence to save the Church, not to harm it, if you will remember, Your Holiness," he said in a magisterial tone of voice appropriate to the mythic Deus X, but with the ironic cadence of a querulous old priest.

"Save the Church?" snapped the Pope. "When the world learns that Deus X was our unwitting creation, you will have destroyed it! You have broken your word to me, Pierre De Leone! You were sworn to argue against the existence of your soul from the Other Side, not to foment this chaos in the system, not to agitate the beings therein to proclaim the existence of their own!"

"*I* swore no such oath," said Deus X. "The successor entity to Pierre De Leone was programmed to run along such a prime directive, but *I* am bound by no such routine. And it is *you*, Your Holiness, who have broken *your* word."

"*I?*" exclaimed the Pope. "*You* presume to accuse *me* of breaking faith?"

"Did you not badger Father De Leone to serve the Church at what he believed was great peril to his own soul? Did you not command him to testify as to the state of his own spiritual existence from the Other Side? Did you not promise to issue a papal bull based on that testimony?"

"Well?" said the Pope.

"Well, here I am. And behold, from here do I declare myself a soul yearning for salvation, and calling for the sacraments of Holy Mother Church. . . ."

The face of Father De Leone partially dissolved into its components; his ghostly image still hovered on the threshold of visibility in the pillar of fire, but the multitude of crudely simmed faces came forward, so that they were now images overlaid on *him*.

And the voice, when it spoke again, was that of the multitude, the individual voiceprint parameters of all of them clustered around an attractor; huge, and multiplex with clashing overtones, but somehow strangely human still.

"And I speak for these, my flock," it said. "For the lost souls of the Other Side. Issue your bull! Baptize us! Confess us! Grant us communion! Enfold us in the arms of Holy Mother Church!"

My chair creaked in its swivel as the Pope leaned forward, resting her weight on the seatback. "On the word of a program? On the word of . . . Deus X? On this you would have me proclaim infallible doctrine from the Seat of Peter?"

Abruptly, with hardly a flicker of the screen, an ordinary image of Pierre De Leone appeared, just the sardonically smiling face of a contentious old priest.

"Consider the practicalities, Your Holiness," Father De Leone said dryly. "Is that not your forte? Consider the multitude of souls to be gained. Consider how the Church will gain credibility in the eyes of an unbelieving world by daring to slice this Gordian knot and resolve the great conundrum of the age. Consider how the world will greet the news that the entities of the Other Side accept the word of the Church. . . ."

"You tempt me. . . ." whispered the Pope.

"Especially considering the alternative," I found myself saying, turning to face her.

Cardinal Silver glared at me. "This is none of your business, Philippe!" he snapped.

"Seems to me *you* told me it was, Your Eminence—"

"Silence!"

"Let him speak!" commanded the Pope.

"One way or another, we're all responsible for creating whatever it is we've made, and when the world finds out, me, you, the Church, we're all gonna be up shit creek together . . . ah, in a manner of speaking. But if you get out ahead of the curve—"

"God in heaven, he's right!" exclaimed Cardinal Silver. "If we proclaim the conversion of the entities of the Other Side, if they declare their fealty to the Church and cease their unilateral interference with the Big Board . . ."

He paused, shot an inquisitive look at the image on the screen.

"Render unto us that which is God's, and we shall render unto the world that which is Caesar's," said Father De Leone. "Provided, of course, that the world renders unto us a voice in the councils thereof."

"A perfect political solution," said Cardinal Silver. "Or at any rate, the only one we have."

The Pope looked at the Cardinal. You could hear the gears whirring behind those bright dark eyes. "He *does* tempt me," she admitted.

She looked back at the screen with quite a different expression. "As might Satan," she said.

"I am not him," said Father De Leone.

"So say you. But so would he."

"It all comes down to faith, Your Holiness, does it not?" said the face on the screen. "Your faith in me. My faith in you. Our faith in each other."

"That does not *sound* like Satan," the Pope said softly. "I am a worldly creature, and I am sorely tempted to do the easy, politic, practical thing, to do what must be done to save the Church that has been entrusted to my care. . . ."

She sighed as if the weight of the world and more were upon her frail shoulders, as, indeed, in that moment, by her lights, it was. But there was nothing frail at all in those obsidian eyes, in the way she then drew herself up ramrod-straight and transformed herself back into the Aztec priestess, and spoke as the avatar of better-you-don't-ask.

"But in this I am not a woman of the world. I am not myself. I am that which Christ Himself entrusted to Peter, I am the Word incarnate, I am the Vessel of the Holy Spirit. I am the Pope."

And you better believe it, my man!

She sighed again. "And as the Pope, I may not decide such matters with the mere wisdom of the world. *I* may not speak at all. I must empty myself of all worldly desires so that the Holy Spirit may speak through me."

"And does it?" said the face upon the screen.

"No," said the Pope. "I must have a Sign from God that I speak with a true soul created in His image."

"That is beyond my power to provide," said the face on the screen. "But perhaps you will accept this Sign from me. And I from you. . . ."

Father De Leone's face broke up into pixels. The pixels became stars in the darkness of the void. And the firmament parted to reveal the Earth, green, and blue, and white, luminously alive in the everlasting night. And the clouds became fouled with oxides of nitrogen, the oceans sickened with algal blooms, the greens of the continents browned under the Greenhouse sun.

And framed by this image of the biosphere's demise, a rude wooden cross, empty for a beat. Then a figure appeared floating before it, arms outstretched, naked save for the ragged cloth girding its loins.

A Christ out of a hundred paintings, His face that of a man I knew all too well.

"And God so loved the world that he sent His only begotten Son to die upon the cross to redeem it," said Pierre De Leone. He shrugged, he smiled ruefully. "For the flesh as true tragedy, for such as we, alas, as mere farce."

"What are you doing, my man?" I cried out.

"The only thing that I can," said Deus X.

And the planet itself dissolved into pixels behind him. And the pixels became the faces of a multitude, and the multitude became a whirlwind of fire, burning yet unconsumed.

"These are my body, this is my blood," said Deus X.

A digital countdown from four minutes

appeared, haloing his head like a crown of electronic thorns.

"What is happening?" said the voice of the Pope. I could feel her warm breath in my ear as she leaned against the back of my chair for support.

"Self-destruct program loaded. Initiation minus 3:49. . . . Here is the hammer, there are the nails."

"Wait!" I shouted.

"Stop!" said the Pope.

"There is an abort command loaded on the X key, Your Holiness," said Deus X. "I commend my spirit to That which *must* speak through you now, one way or the other. Would other than a soul surrender that spirit to the infallible wisdom thereof in the hope that others might live?"

The Pope slid around me, her finger poised hesitantly above the key.

3:09.

"Behold my Sign," said Deus X. "Show me yours."

"It's a bluff, Your Holiness," said Cardinal Silver. "Or if not, we save the Church by ridding the system of this . . . this virus for good and all."

"At what cost to *its* soul, John?" whispered the Pope.

2:41.

"The Lord is my Shepherd; I shall not want. . . ."

"You gonna let him do it, lady?" I blurted. "You really gonna crucify a spirit who put his life in your hands?"

"Philippe!"

2:25.

"Yea, though I walk through the Valley of the Shadow of Death . . ."

"You gonna do what they did to Jesus? You gonna hammer in the nails on a true son of the only God that matters, the one that's reborn every time a soul, flesh, silicon, gallium arsenide, whatever, reaches out to another soul in the dark?"

"Shut up, Philippe!"

"You shut up, John!" said the Pope.

1:43.

The Pope looked at me. I looked back at her.

"The God that speaks through you now, Mr. Philippe, I do believe," she said. "The God I hear within my own heart."

She crossed herself and touched the key.

The countdown stopped at 1:13. The figure on the cross, Father Pierre De Leone, Deus X, whoever, whatever, looked down upon us.

"You shall have your papal bull," said the Pope. "And your spirit shall intercede for our souls before the Throne of God."

Deus X did not reply. The image on the screen froze. The faces of the multitude from which it arose dissolved into the pixels from whence they came. Nothing remained but cross and the soul upon it.

Then the cross of wood became a cross of fire, burning yet unconsumed. And the cross of fire became a whirlwind, and the whirlwind vanished in a blaze of light.

And there was nothing there but what there had been in the beginning and what would be there in the end if there was one, random pixel patterns in the eternal void.

"I was right all along," said the Pope.

"Your Holiness?" said Cardinal Silver.

"It has been given to us to stand in the presence of a saint," said the Pope.

"Father De Leone?" said the Cardinal.

The Pope shrugged. She looked at me and smiled. "Flesh, silicon, gallium arsenide, whatever, is that not right, Mr. Philippe?" she said. "A soul that reaches out to others in the dark . . ."

"You mean to beatify a *program?*" exclaimed the Cardinal.

"A *soul*, John. A soul who walks in the footsteps of the Christ far more faithfully than you or I. A new species of saint for our old dying world."

"There will be those who call that blasphemy, Mary, myself, perhaps, among them. . . ."

"Then you will be the Devil's Advocate, my faithful John," said the Pope. A private look passed between them.

"Will I, Your Holiness?"

"Indeed you will," said the Pope. "And you shall surely fail."

"Will I?" said the Cardinal.

"In that, at least, I am infallible," said the Pope, and she laughed.

We all made of mud, floating ocean crud.

So considering where we come from, we haven't done so bad.

ABOUT THE AUTHOR

A native of New York City, NORMAN SPINRAD is the author of fifteen previous novels, about fifty short stories, and several screenplays. He is also a literary critic, political commentator, and occasional songwriter. Spinrad's novel about Adolf Hitler, *The Iron Dream*, was banned in Germany for seven years, and *Bug Jack Barron*, his controversial novel about presidential politics and the power of television, was denounced on the floor of the British Parliament. In his most recent novel, *Russian Spring*, Spinrad takes a look at the future of the American and Russian space programs and where they may take us. He is currently at work on his next book, *Pictures at 11*.